Maggie McIntyre is Living the Dream

Joanne Nicholson

Contents

Transformation

Dream Time

Awakened

Sleep In

Shattered Dreams

Model in the Making

Dream Come True

FLEA MARKET

Who doesn't love a flea market? Someone's trash is another person's treasure and all that! Everyone, deep down, loves to find a good bargain. Everyone, that is, except Jason. With hindsight, maybe that should have been my first warning sign, quickly followed by the fact that his mother could never get my name right. Is Maggie really all that hard to remember? She called me Margie, Margot, Marge, Margaret and I'm pretty sure she even once called me Maggot.

Of course, I kick myself now for my naivety. I thought innocently leaving Tiffany & Co catalogues scattered around the apartment with a big red circle drawn around the diamond solitaire was a discreet hint to Jason that I would be open to a proposal. After a while, I reduced my expectations to a cubic zirconia from Pandora, but it seemed I hadn't lowered my expectations enough.

Jason went on a month-long sabbatical,

travelling around Australia on his newly purchased Harley Davidson motorbike to find himself. It seems his motorbike found its way to his ex-girlfriend Rosemary's house in Queensland. The same ex-girlfriend who, when given an ultimatum from him to choose him or her cat, had promptly trashed the house and then left him, never to be seen again. Or so I thought. It turns out she had called him after she found herself in some trouble and being the knight in shining armour that he was, he rushed to her side and arranged for her to move back to live with him.

I'd hoped while travelling he would have the epiphany that what he needed was what was waiting at home for him. The only proposal I received when he returned was that he could help me cover a bond payment so that I could move out ASAP.

At first, I'd done some pleading and ugly crying – you know the sort where snot runs out of your nose, like some dam up there has broken, and tears drip off your chin. It was so bad that when I went to open my phone, it wouldn't recognise my face. I'd ranted at the phone that it couldn't be serious, to which Siri responded she was listening. I took my frustration out on Jason, yelling at him that he was a dick. Siri promptly provided me with a list of websites for penis enlargement. Jason had the decency to at least look bad, or maybe on reflection, he just looked awkward.

Jason grabbed my hand, and I'd thought he was going to change his mind. Instead, he told me that he'd never really gotten over Rosemary and that he had to follow his heart. He then offered to organise a removalist to move my things out of his apartment within a fortnight. I'd held my head high and told him I didn't need his charity. The truth of the matter was that I only owned the double bed in the spare room and a retro table in the kitchen that had mismatched wooden chairs painted different colours with flecks of missing paint that gave the set a worn, well-loved look. I thought they were charming. Jason had always suggested the setting belonged at the tip.

My dad had arrived towing his rusty old box-trailer and shifted my bed, table and chairs to a small one-bedroom villa I had managed to find at short notice. I threw my meager belongings into a suitcase and then subtly left an old Valentine's Day card in my bedside drawer. It was one I'd received my first year with Jason, with a picture of two puppies kissing, where Jason had written that he loved me more than anything in the world. I knew Jason would never check that drawer, but just like a dog, I wanted to mark my territory before I left.

I had stalked his ex-girlfriend, or more correctly,

since I was now the ex, his current girlfriend's Facebook mercilessly. After squirrelling down into her friends' accounts, I saw her tagged in photos and posts with more than one name. She had five aliases – Rose, Rosemary, Posie, Trixie and, my favourite, Kween. Seriously, unless you're on the run from the mafia, who needs multiple aliases? I conjured up an image of her as a spider, wrapping Jason in light silk thread, making him feel secure until it reached a point that she had wound him up so tightly that he couldn't move, at which time she would bite off his head. I would never have thought Jason was capable of cheating on me, particularly with an ex who seemed a bit unstable, but then again, I guess I never really knew Jason.

Anyway, I digress. This morning I set out to walk to my local farmers' markets, to purchase a freshly made green smoothie and then walk aimlessly around the adjacent flea market. I had woken at the reasonable hour of 9am and walked the whole way to the markets. It may have only been two blocks from my place, but nonetheless I walked the whole way, an honourable task for someone who hasn't walked any reasonable distance, since I was supposed to be running cross country in high school. Even then, I took short cuts and hid in bushes, before strolling across the finish line somewhere in the middle of the pack. It should have been a dead giveaway that I'd cheated, when everyone else had bright red faces and were ready to cough up a lung. I hoped I'd pass as being fit, and that's why I looked like I hadn't exerted myself.

As much as I'd planned on purchasing a healthy green drink, in reality I had ordered a banana smoothie, because honestly I hate the thought of kale or any other leafy vegetable, getting pulverized into a drink. But it is the thought that counts, and I did think about having a green juice. Plus, the honey in the banana smoothie was organic and so I felt semi-wholesome knowing that I was supporting busy bees that are free to suck on the dandelions that I purposely let grow in my yard as a treat for them. It was a symbiotic relationship, which frankly was the only type of relationship I currently had.

Sucking on my smoothie, I wandered around the stalls in the flea market. The air smelt of a mixture of incense, mothballs and coffee. To my delight, I spied a not too tattered vinyl record of Elton John's *Honky Chateau* and a vinyl 45 of The Proclaimers' *I'm gonna be (500 miles)*. After paying $15 for my highly collectable vinyl records, I continued to dawdle around the stalls. One day I would have to invest in a record player to play the albums. Ignoring the tie-dyed clothing and crocheted baby clothes, I found a new-age stall offering an eclectic mix of bits and pieces. The smokey aroma of incense cloyed in the back of my throat, signaling they must be legitimately new age. I picked up a Tibetan singing bowl and although I tried my best to make it sing, rubbing the brass donger around the bowl, it remained stubbornly mute. I then wandered over to a display of Himalayan salt lamps. Personally, I prefer salt on my food, not a lump of it glowing on my bedside table. Further along was an array of crystals with tags that described their powers. I was a veritable kid in a candy shop. After perusing the crystals, I couldn't decide what I needed. With some assistance from the shopkeeper, a woman with flowing black hair, wearing a colourful moo-moo (who ever came up with that as a name for a piece of fashion must have been smoking something strong), I ended up choosing crystals for peace, love and happiness and then threw in one for protection, because, why not? As the sales assistant moved to retrieve a small hessian sack to hold my crystals, my eyes landed on the most magnificent looking dream catcher hanging at the back of the stall. According to the stallholder, it was an authentic American Indian artifact, not some mass-produced item you could buy on eBay. It had beautiful brown and black eagle feathers dangling from the hand woven centre. I knew it would make the perfect decoration in my dull office, so without hesitation I handed over the last of my cash and carefully carried my new purchases home.

DREAM JOB

When I completed school at the age of eighteen, I was full of dreams and aspirations. My parents were so proud that I had been accepted into university to complete a degree in psychology. It only took me eighteen months of arduous study to find out that a three-year degree in psychology qualifies you to do not much at all. Only with a master's degree and/or a doctorate and with the appropriate hours of clinical training, would I be able to practice as a qualified psychologist. I would then also need to undertake additional education every year to retain my qualifications. I hated academia and realized at that point that maybe some level of investigation should have been undertaken before I chose my selected degree. I knew with certainty that I didn't want to continue at university, but given the fact I was already halfway through my undergraduate degree I decided to finish it and then look into interesting career options.

Sometimes when you're not looking, opportunities leap up and hit you square in the face. My career path was one of those moments. Feeling horrendously hung over one morning, I was sitting chatting with my friend Kayleigh's flat mate, who worked at the local radio station. He was relaying his dream. If there is one thing in life that most people hate, it's having to listen to people rambling on about the nonsense that was the dream they had the night before. Being polite, I was nodding along, as I was zoned out thinking about the calories in a McDonalds Big Mac and whether those calories counted if it was for medicinal purposes of curing my hangover. Before I knew it, Kayleigh had dumped me in the deep end, proclaiming that as a psychology undergraduate, I was qualified to interpret dreams. Brought out of my reverie, while shooting silent death stares at Kayleigh, I listened to the tail end of her flat mate's monotonous dream. Piecing together a few well-worn psychological phrases that I trotted out regularly for essays and talking utter bullshit, I 'analysed' his dream. The resulting effect was that he was blown away by my interpretation of his dreams and within a week I had received an email from his work, asking whether I would consider being their resident dream analyst with a weekly spot on their breakfast show. Twenty percent of me thought it was unethical to pretend I knew about dreams while eighty percent couldn't believe what a great opportunity it would be to work in a radio station.

I jumped online and Googled the hell out of every dream scenario, animal, feeling and location I could think of and then created a dream reference spreadsheet. I even went so far as to purchase a book called 'Keys to your Dreams' and memorized the significant sections. I figured I would use these cues and intersperse some psychological terms. You know, basically baffle them with waffle.

The first time my dream analysing segment ran, the station was inundated with people wanting to make sense of their weird and wonderful dreams. Surprisingly, I found that I had absorbed the dream interpretations and had fun with the segment. The callers all decreed I was eerily accurate. In short, I was a runaway success. Within a month, a teen magazine had also approached me to be a regular contributor and it all somehow snowballed into me creating a business called 'Day Dream,' resulting in me opening an office to take appointments to do personal appraisals of people's dream diaries.

My office was a dingy, shoebox of a space, located on the first floor, above a strip of shops. I had never been prouder than the moment I saw my name on the door of my office. In silver script it read 'Day Dream Inc, Maggie McIntyre,

BPsychSc.' I took a photo and sent it to Kayleigh. She rang me immediately in a fit of hysterics. I'd been so focused on the lettering on the door, I had missed that there was a faint trace of a sticky residue from the sign of the previous tenant, which had the words sleep clinic directly under my name. I sprayed and wiped the hell out of the door until it gleamed, leaving no trace of the preceding business. The previous tenant had been three months in arrears with rent and had locked the doors and done a runner in the middle of the night a month before I was looking for the space. They had left a grey melamine desk, a dodgy office chair with a minor rip in the fabric on the seat, a rusty old grey filing cabinet, a vinyl visitor's seat and a mug with a new furry green habitat growing on the surface of three-month-old coffee. In my hard-hitting negotiations with the real estate agent, I asked for the furniture to remain for my use, but politely requested the mug disappear.

It was around this time that I first met Jason. He was in his mid thirties with thinning blonde hair and pale blue eyes. He owned the computer repair shop below my office and seemed like a nice, normal guy. The moment he heard my name and what I did for a living, he recognised me from the radio station. I think in hindsight he may have been a bit star-struck, thinking I was famous. I was just happy to have found someone that seemed to like me regardless of the fact I was curvaceous (that is code for: I consumed too many fast food meals and cheap alcoholic beverages while at university). In my opinion, I had the perfect look for radio.

Our first date was at the all you can eat buffet at the local RSL, washed down with sweet pink Moscato. He wined me and dined me and when he told me I was his 'dream girl' I thought he was sincere, not realising it was just a corny pun on my chosen career. Without any spoken understanding, we ended up at his apartment and let's just say I made his dreams come true. Within the month, I had moved a suitcase of clothes into his wardrobe, deposited my anti-frizz shampoo in his shower and put my double bed in the spare room so we could host guests. I also insisted on having my little contribution to the household aesthetic by wedging my cute retro dining setting into his kitchen. Hindsight is a funny thing. I now realise I was never actually officially invited to move in with Jason. Like a lot of our relationship it was an unspoken assumption which confirms the adage that when you assume something it just makes an ass out of you and me.

DREAM CATCHER

My business had grown steadily, and I had enough clients to pay my rent on the office and the villa, pay bills and have a small amount left over to save. I mean hypothetically save, because realistically things like eyelash extensions and a gym membership that I was definitely going to start using one day, seemed to chew up my savings.

One frosty Monday morning, I dressed in woolen tweed check pants, a singlet, skivvy and jumper before wrapping a scarf around my neck and donning a coat. The office heating was dodgy at best, non-existent at worst. As my grandfather would say, it was so cold in the office, it would freeze the balls off a brass monkey. I'm not sure who actually owned a brass monkey that was anatomically correct, but that is beside the point. My office was as close to being in a refrigerator that a human could be.

Looking mummified in all the layers, I carried my new dream catcher into the office and as I didn't own a hammer, I improvised with the heel of my shoe, to nail in a picture hook and hung my magnificent authentic American Indian dream catcher on the wall behind my desk. Satisfied that it was the perfect decoration for my office, I sat down to write that month's column for *Teen Girl*, before getting ready for my first appointment of the day.

At 10am on the dot, a knock on the door alerted me that Daisy had arrived for her appointment. She had regular monthly appointments and in that time had journaled every dream she could recall. Making small talk prior to getting into each month's dream analysis, I had managed to glean that Daisy was a bit of a loner. She was your archetypical crazy cat lady, who had a heart of gold but felt lonely and misunderstood. This insight made it easy to 'interpret' her dreams.

Daisy sat in the vinyl visitor's chair. She had been often enough to know there was no point in removing her coat when inside.

'How are you today Daisy?' I asked.

'Not too bad. I really like your new thing on the wall.'

'It's an authentic American Indian dream

catcher. They are eagle feathers hanging down below.'

'I wonder how an eagle flies without its feathers?' Daisy mused. I didn't have the heart to tell her I thought the eagle that had donated its feathers was probably dead.

'The Indians believed dream catchers protect people from bad dreams. It catches the good dreams and then they flow down the feathers to the person below.'

'That's interesting. Maybe I should get one, so I only have good dreams,' Daisy said wistfully.

'I think most of your dreams are pretty good, Daisy. Even the ones that on the surface may seem bad, may actually in fact be a sign of change or something good.'

'Well I did have a really good dream the other night.' Daisy opened her diary and scanned until she found the page she was searching for. 'I was at home, except it wasn't my actual home, but in the dream, it was my home. It had all sorts of mismatched furniture, like it had all come from an op shop, but it felt homely and comfortable. I was at the dining setting where every seat was a different colour. I was sitting on the orange chair which is funny because I don't really like orange. It's a colour that clashes with my red hair.'

Externally I nodded while in my mind I willed her to get to the point.

'Anyway, this big grey cat jumped up on my windowsill. In my dream I didn't have any pets, so I wondered where the cat had come from and who owned it. I put out a saucer of milk for the cat and it lapped it up until it had drunk the whole amount. It was purring madly, it was so happy. I put it in a wicker basket and carried it out onto the street and I walked for miles trying to find its owner. It started to get dark and so I had to take it home. I made it a cosy bed in the basket with a blanket that my dear old mum had knitted.' Daisy interrupted her dream recall. 'That is a real blanket that I have in the top of my cupboard that my mum made when I was about thirty. It's blue and orange and doesn't go with anything in my house, but I cherish it because she made it with love.'

I nodded again and jotted a note down on the blank notebook in front of me – blanket made with love.

'Anyway, in my dream, I woke up the next morning and the cat had a litter of kittens and they were all mewing away. There were three grey kittens and one little runt that was ginger. The mother cat was licking the ginger cat tenderly.'

I jotted another note – ginger cat gets attention.

'The next thing I knew the doorbell rang, and I was flustered because I was in my pyjamas and I didn't want to answer the door dressed like that, but I didn't want the person to go away.' Daisy laughed. 'I was torn between having a shower and getting dressed or just putting on something to cover up my pyjamas. I put on my Dad's old army trench coat to answer the door and it was a man in a bright red jumper who said he was there for his cat. I told him the cat had given birth to a litter of kittens. He picked up the basket and then passed the ginger kitten to me, saying he didn't want the runt. I was so angry that he abandoned the kitten, so I kicked him in the shins and demanded he at least give me back my basket and blanket. He then walked out with the mother cat and the three grey kittens in his arms. The mother cat was crying because she was leaving her kitten behind. I patted the mother cat's head and whispered to her that I would look after her baby and she nodded and then I woke up.'

'Okay, that's an interesting dream Daisy. I'll break it down for you. Cats in dreams symbolize your independent spirit and intuition. The fact that this cat came to you to have her kittens represents that you are someone who can be trusted to protect something you care about. Giving the cat your cherished blanket that your mother made indicates that you have a mothering instinct, which materialized as this cat becoming a mother. I believe the little ginger runt is a manifestation of you, given that you have red hair. Just as the mother cat bonded with the ginger cat, you have a precious relationship with your own mum. You have mentioned before that you see yourself as being different to other people and this kitten too was different to the other kittens. I thought it was interesting that when you went to open the door that you put on your father's overcoat. Didn't your father leave when you were a child? I think the choice of clothing was a pre-cursor to the fact that someone of authority was going to come and destroy the cat's family unit. The little ginger cat was abandoned, just as your father abandoned you when you were young. You could sense the mother's devotion to her kitten but also the fact that she was torn as she needed to look after the rest of her family. Do you sometimes feel that your mum is torn between looking after you and listening to the rest of the family who think you are a bit of an oddball?'

Daisy had tears glistening in her eyes. 'Yes,' she answered in a small voice.

I felt bad for upsetting Daisy, but she had come to me looking for answers. I placed my hand over her hand that was resting on my desk. 'You know that you have a heart full of love to give and you know that your mum will always look out for you. That is why the blanket is so important in the dream. The man was wearing a red jumper because red is the colour of danger. You know, like a red stop sign or a red fire engine.'

Daisy nodded in agreement.

'Anyway, you knew this man was in danger of upsetting the family situation, but this dream shows that you know that it is okay to be different because you freely adopted the little ginger kitten. It wasn't hurt or injured in the altercation. It was just discarded and handed to you. You knew the mother cat was sad, but you showed that you could look after the ginger kitten, which translates into knowing that you can look after yourself, because as I said before the ginger cat is a representation of you. Daisy, you know that you are different; you know that your mum loves you and you acknowledge that your father abandoned you. At the end of the day, this dream is reinforcing that you know that you will be alright.'

Daisy nodded and grinned widely. 'You are a genius, Maggie. I've gone to years of counseling, trying to come to terms with my dad leaving and blaming myself because I'm different to my family.

In this one session you've shown me that my mum loves me unconditionally, that it is okay that my dad left and more importantly that I'm going to be fine.'

I laughed. 'Daisy, I haven't told you that. Your dreams did. You just need to listen to your inner intuition and believe in your independent spirit. After all, that's why the dream came through in the form of cats.'

'That's bloody brilliant. You deserve a Nobel peace prize,' Daisy said, walking around to my side of the desk to wrap me in a bear hug.

I was torn between feeling elated that I had helped Daisy so much, because that was why I had originally gone into my psychology degree, and feeling awkward as she was cramping my personal space as she crushed me to her bosom in her coat that smelt musty and was covered in white cat's fur.

After tidying up some loose ends at work, I decided to give myself an early mark. I had resolved to clean my home. I like to think of myself as a cup is half full kind of gal, so the great thing about living in a one bedroom villa that is the size of a Kardashian walk-in robe, scratch that, it's more like half the size of a Kardashian walk-in robe, is the fact that it takes next to no time to clean. My PB for vacuuming the house is four minutes and twenty-five seconds. All I have in the way of furniture is my very cool retro kitchen table and chairs, a two seater lounge that is more shabby than chic, a coffee table made of pallets that someone two doors down put outside for a council pick up and my sad little double bed in my bedroom. I find it quite cathartic to clean, so with that in mind and aiming for a new vacuuming PB, I whizzed around the house cleaning like a maniac. The bathroom was the most time-consuming area as I always seemed to have some gunky build up of hair and god-knows-what that I had to fish out of the shower drain. My shower screen also seemed to build up an incredibly thick layer of soap residue. I've made the assumption that it comes from my shampoo. The bottle should read, 'guaranteed to leave you with smooth silky hair and to frost your shower screen in an opaque scum in two washes or your money back.' I'm actually grateful for the need to use elbow grease to clean the shower, as it's the only work out my tuck shop lady arms get. One of these days I will absolutely start to use my gym membership.

With my house sparkling, I took out the rubbish to put it in my wheelie bin. When I opened the lid to the bin, I was shocked to find that some mysterious person has been topping up my bin with their rubbish. Tied in a lavender scented, purple plastic bin liner, a whole bag of trash was nestled in my bin, leaving me only a small space to try to cram in my own garbage. Gritting my teeth and grunting under my breath, I vowed I would make it my mission to find the lavender bin thief. Okay, maybe they're not a thief as they didn't steal the bin, but they stole my space in the bin without getting my permission first. I refuse to let people dispose of their refuse in my bin!

I wheeled my bulging bin out onto the street, as it was thankfully bin collection night. After doing so I heard a soft sound, like a kid's toy that has run low on batteries that just makes a whining noise. It was bad enough that they had used my bin, but to throw out noisy rubbish was a step too far! I stepped up to the bin to try to find the offending toy. I removed my own rubbish and tore open the purple bag. To my shock and dismay, something moved. I screamed in a panic and dropped the lid down.

Curiosity got the better of me, so with shaking hands, I slowly pried the lid of the bin open again. I was terrified it was a rat in the rubbish, but I had to see for myself. On top of a pile of rags, was a poor little innocent kitten that was surely not even a day old. It was blindly waving its head around in search of its mother as it mewed quietly. I plucked the poor little creature out of the rubbish and wrapped it inside my cardigan. I was shocked that it was still alive. What sort of sick person throws out a helpless kitten like a piece of rubbish? My annoyance had bubbled up into pure rage. If I ever caught that lavender scented piece of scum, they would rue the day they had messed with the little ginger cat and me.

'Shhhh. It's going to be okay,' I cooed to the kitten. The kitten just tried to nestle in closer to me, still searching for its elusive mother. 'I'm going to take you to the vet and get you some food.'

I found a little wicker breadbasket and lined it with an odd sock that I had lying around. I'm not entirely sure how my socks get separated. I wear two socks, I put two socks out to be washed and then only one sock makes it through the wash. The other one, more often than not, seems to evaporate into thin air. I keep a collection of my odd socks with the hope that one day their pairs will miraculously reappear and be reunited. Anyway, this odd sock had particular sentimental value as it was from my days playing in the university quidditch team. A purple and orange striped wooly sock was the perfect lining to keep my furry friend warm while I took her to the vet.

Driving to the closest vet, I realized that the kitten didn't have a name and they would have to create a file for it. Racking my brain, I mumbled name options to myself as I drove. My first line of thought was a play on the fact that it was a little ginger kitten. 'Ginger Megs' – maybe, 'Ginger Beer' – nope, 'Ginger Vitus' – definitely not. I decided to change tack, and that's when it hit me. 'Lady Marmalade' or 'Marmalade' for short, or 'Marmie' for shorter or even 'Marm' for the shortest. Hearing Marmie crying was heartbreaking, but as we neared the vet, she went quiet, and no noise was far more frightening.

'Not far now. Hang in there, Marmie.'

I had my seatbelt off and had barely put the car in park when I grabbed the basket and ran towards the vet door. I frantically dinged on the little brass bell that sat on the unattended reception desk.

'Hello? I need help. Is anyone here?' I called out into the void of the vet surgery.

A man stuck his head around the doorway. They say that pets resemble their owners, but this vet looked like he had morphed into a conglomeration of all animals. He had the hangdog eyes of a hound, a wild curly mop of white hair like a poodle, two big bucky teeth like a beaver and the lean build of a greyhound. 'Can I help?' he asked.

'It's an emergency. I found this little kitten

discarded in a rubbish bag in my garbage bin. She was crying, but she has stopped. Please help her.'

I thrust the basket into his hands. He plucked the kitten out from under my sock and it began to move its head around weakly. 'Firstly, let's get some milk into her, and then I can assess her. Do you know how long she was in the bin?'

I looked at him. Did he think after I found her in the bin, I left her there for a while and then thinking better of it a few days later pulled it out? Of course, I had no idea how long it had been there, or for that matter, the identity of the evil monster who had put her there. 'No,' I replied, 'but I found her half an hour ago and then I came here.'

The vet mixed up some formula milk and with an eyedropper dispensed it into the kitten's mouth. Like nectar from the Gods, Marmie greedily gulped down the milk. I took over feeding duties while the vet got his stethoscope to listen to the kitten's heart. He then felt her body for any signs of injury. Within ten minutes he was convinced that the kitten would be fine. He then led me back to reception and handed me a tin of cat milk formula. 'Feed her three times a day. The directions are on the tin.'

'Thank you so much. You saved her life,' I said, tenderly stroking the little kitten's head.

'I'll just fill out the paperwork,' the vet said as he wriggled a mouse on his computer that resembled a real mouse. I love a bit of quirkiness. 'What's your name, the cat's name and date of birth.'

'I'm Maggie McIntyre, and my date of birth is 24th August 1988, and this is Lady Marmalade.' Lady Marmalade McIntyre sounded posh, even downright royal. I was very happy with my choice of name.

The vet looked at me and smirked. 'I was actually after the cat's date of birth.'

I laughed. 'Oh, um, do you think she was born today?'

'Probably. I'll just put that,' he said, typing away. He then printed out a piece of paper and handed it to me. 'Okay. That will be $165 for today,' the vet said, smiling with his bucky beaver grin.

I gulped. What. The. Actual. Hell? I pulled my credit card out of my purse and handed it over. It looked like I wasn't going to be adding to my savings again this month. It's a strange world where you don't choose to have a pet and then suddenly it is thrust upon you and instantly starts costing you money. It's also a strange world where within minutes of saving an innocent little kitten it has already wriggled its way deep into your heart.

I couldn't leave Lady Marmalade at home by herself, so I tucked her in her breadbasket bed and took her to the shops with me. I'd had to replace the Quidditch sock with another odd sock after the basket began dripping warm, wet liquid onto my lap on the way home. It was probably a bit short-sighted of me to not realise that after drinking milk little Marmie was going to have to relieve herself. I quickly changed and then drove straight to K-Mart and bought a cat bed, litter tray, a ribbon on a stick and food bowls for when she was old enough to eat real food. I wasn't sure when that was, but with the help of Google, I was sure I would be able to become an instant expert on all feline things.

When I was stopped by security on my way out to see what I was hiding in the basket, mini mayhem broke out. The shop assistant squealed with delight at my new companion and within a minute Marmie had a fan club of people swarming around her, all stroking her head and cooing at her. I had to draw a line when someone tried to pick her up. Marmie had had a stressful enough day, without being handed around from one stranger to another. 'She hasn't been immunized so you can't pick her up. I really have to take her home to sleep now,' I said, pushing my way through the crowd.

I placed her basket on my lap to drive home. It was probably short-sighted of me to not think that she might need to pee more than once a day. When I got home, I placed her into her new, big (by this I mean small, but big in comparison to her) fluffy bed and changed into my third set of clothing for the day.

DREAM ON

My first job for the day was to ring the radio station and analyse dreams for their listeners. I truly hoped I didn't get a caller telling me the stock standard dream of flying. Almost every week I had to listen patiently and then tell the person that it represented freedom. If they were regular listeners, they should have already known that, but yet they continued to call with the same boring themes. I just wished for once someone would have an interesting and original dream.

I hadn't slept well the night before, as I was worried about Marmie. I had placed her on the litter tray before retiring for the night, but I was still concerned that she would wet the bedding, wander off or climb out a window. I know it's irrational to think a baby kitten could possibly climb out a window, but at 2am thoughts wander and conjure up a list of issues that a mind that's not foggy with sleep can process as ludicrous.

Sitting at my desk, I glanced down to the little orange ball of fluff that was sleeping peacefully in her bed next to me. I couldn't help myself but lightly stroke her fur. I had never even really liked cats, so the fact that I was swept up in the cuteness overload of this little creature was a mystery to me.

Just as I called the radio station, Marmalade opened her eyes and began crying. I tried to muffle the sound by placing my hand over the phone receiver.

'What's that noise?' the producer asked.

'Sorry, it's my new kitten. Someone abandoned her and left her to die in my garbage bin,' I said as I rooted around trying to find the bottle of formula I had pre-made.

'That's dreadful,' the producer responded. 'Hey, it's a slow news day today. Why don't you bring the kitten to the studio? We can push back your segment and then do a story on the cat before you do your dream analysing.'

With the phone wedged between my shoulder and ear, and a crying hangry kitten on my lap, I was quick to agree, just so I could get off the phone and feed Marmalade.

When I arrived at the radio station, it was like I

was a rock star. I was mobbed as people vied to get access to little Lady Marmalade. Thankfully she was happy to get passed around getting pats from all the staff. Eventually I was ushered into the studio booth.

As I placed the oversized headphones over my ears, Charlie, the female announcer, took Marmie. 'Oh my God, I'm a natural. Look at this bundle of adorableness. For those of you just tuning in, Maggie McIntyre, our resident dream analyst, has brought in her new kitten. It is a stripy ginger fluff ball, that if I hold it close enough to the mic, you might be able to hear it purring. What's her name?'

'I called her Lady Marmalade,' I replied. Within a second, a sound bite of the song Lady Marmalade began to play.

'Isn't she the cutest thing you've ever seen Davey?'

'I'm more of a dog person to be honest,' Davey replied. 'So Maggie, tell us what made you get a kitten, because, just for the record dogs are better.'

I laughed. 'Well Davey, I didn't choose to get a kitten; the kitten sort of got dumped on me. I found Marmalade in a purple plastic bin liner that someone had discarded in my bin. At first I thought it was a rat.'

Davey laughed. 'For the listeners at home, let me tell you it does look a bit like a rat.'

'Davey, don't be mean about my new best friend,' Charlie chimed in.

'Once I realized it was a kitten, I took her to the vet for the once over. She's a fighter. I just can't believe that anyone in society could do something so cruel.'

'I've never trusted people who use purple bin liners. I think that choice of colour says something about people. What's wrong with a plain white liner? Only weird people choose coloured bin liners.'

'Oh, I don't know about that. I use yellow bin liners,' Charlie replied.

'Thanks for proving my statement that only weird people choose coloured bin liners,' Davey said playfully.

'Ignore him people,' Charlie said into the microphone whilst still gently stroking Marmalade's fur. 'I think his mother may have dropped him on his head as a child. Anyway, if anyone knows who is responsible for this cold-hearted act, please contact police, RSPCA or call the station.'

'Okay, enough talking about cats.' Davey turned away from Marmie. 'We've got Maggie in here today to do what she does best. So, call us with your dreams and find out what has really been going on in your mind while you sleep.'

'You don't have dreams often, do you Davey?' Charlie asked.

'No, I'm not much of a dreamer,' Davey confirmed.

'Exactly! There's not much going on in that mind when you're awake or asleep,' Charlie quipped.

'Ha ha. You're so hilarious, Charlie,' Davey replied sarcastically. 'Okay, we have Yvette on the line. Why don't you tell us your dream?'

'Oh my goodness, I can't believe I got through. I've always wanted to call in, but I've never had the guts. Firstly, I want to say how lovely it is that you have adopted that sweet little kitten Maggie. You have such a big heart.'

'Thank you, Yvette,' I replied. 'So, what was your dream?'

'Well, I was walking along a headland and it was really windy and then the next thing I ran and flapped my arms and suddenly I was flying.'

I plastered a fake smile on my face, whilst the voice in my head kept screaming 'shoot me now.'

'Well Yvette, flying is a very common dream. It shows a sense of freedom, so either you are looking for freedom, or as you were controlling the flying, you are currently feeling a sense of freedom in your home or work life.' It sounded like waffle to my own ears, but this was what I was paid to do.

'Yes, you're right. My work has just cut back my hours, so I guess I will have a bit more free time to do as I want.'

'Now is the perfect opportunity for you to, excuse the pun, 'follow your dreams' and spend your newfound freedom exploring something that has always interested you,' I replied.

'I have been thinking about doing some painting,' Yvette commented.

'A creative outlet like painting is a wonderful way to express yourself,' I added.

'Oh no, I mean, our laundry needs a new coat of paint. I thought I could do that.'

'Well, that would be good to achieve something you've been putting off. Especially since now you have the time and freedom to do that.'

'Thanks for calling Yvette. Now we have Jasper on the line. Jasper, what is your dream?' Davey asked.

'Hey Dude. I had this wicked dream last night that this python was trying to strangle me, and I was wrestling with it.'

'So, Maggie, he was dreaming of wrestling with a snake last night,' Davey said laughing, 'I know lots of guys that choke the snake every day. What does it mean?' Davey was laughing hysterically, making Charlie burst into hysterics too. Little Marmalade awoke from the raucous laughter.

I could feel heat rising in my cheeks. How did I get myself in this situation? 'Hi Jasper. Well, dreaming of snakes relates to dealing with something that you feel is unsettling. Is there something currently in your life that you feel is out of your control?'

'Yeah. My girlfriend dumped me the other day and now she's ghosting me. She's blocked my number, de-friended me on social media and won't answer the door when I go to see her.'

'I'm sorry to hear that,' I said, before Davey interrupted.

'No wonder Jasper's choking the snake since his

girlfriend has left him.' He burst into hysterical laughter again.

'Get your mind out of the gutter, Davey,' I said tersely. I didn't want him to publicly humiliate Jasper.

'Oohh, I'm getting death stares everyone,' Davey said, laughing into the microphone.

'Jasper, as you transition into the new stage of life, you will feel more settled and I expect you won't keep having dreams about pythons. Hang in there. Just remember when one door closes, another door opens.'

'Thanks Maggie,' Jasper said.

'Well, that's all we have time for today. Thanks for coming in Maggie and thank you for bringing in this gorgeous kitten of yours,' Charlie said as Christina Aguilera sang 'Lady Marmalade' in the background.

'Thanks to everyone who called in today and remember to tune in again tomorrow morning from 5.30am for more shenanigans on the Davey and Charlie Breakfast Show.'

Charlie picked up Marmie and held her aloft. 'Ewww, she's just peed all over my lap.'

I rushed around to take my kitten off Charlie. 'Sorry about that. She's not toilet trained yet.' I looked at the wet patch on Charlie's lap and grimaced, although to be honest, a part of me was just grateful the puddle wasn't on my lap for a change.

After leaving the studio, I turned on my phone to find there was a text message from Kayleigh: *I just heard you on the radio – the poor guy about the snake LOL. I can't believe you have a kitten. I'm coming over tonight with wine to wet the head of the baby.*

I quickly shot a text back: *OK, I'll be home by 6pm.*

Back at the office, my day flew by quickly. It was the one day of the week that I didn't take any appointments so I could focus on bookwork and mundane tasks. Marmie slept most of the time, with intermittent breaks for feeding and peeing.

As I drove up my street on my way home that evening, I assessed each person I passed, to judge whether they may be the lavender garbage bag bandit. I vowed the next garbage night to scrutinize the contents of all the bins on my street to see if I could pinpoint who the deranged person was that had abandoned Lady Marmalade.

Once home I had intended on tidying up and making some dinner for Kayleigh and me, but I got distracted waving a ribbon around in front of Marmie. Who knew a cat could be entertained for hours chasing a pink ribbon? Actually, who knew I could be entertained for hours watching a cat chasing a pink ribbon? Before I knew it, the doorbell rang. Clutching Marmie in one hand, I opened the door to find Kayleigh thrusting a bottle of chilled wine at me. I grabbed the bottle as she grabbed Lady Marmalade out of my clutches.

I poured each of us a glass of wine and handed over the ribbon duties to Kayleigh so I could make dinner, and by that I mean, I placed frozen lasagna in the oven and opened a pre-made salad that I put in a bowl.

'So, how are things?' I asked Kayleigh as I took a sip of wine. Marmie walked up to me, so I picked her up and placed her on my lap where she proceeded to knead my legs with her pin-like claws.

'Everything is good. Although I wanted to ask

your advice on what you would do in a situation in which I've found myself.'

I nodded. I loved juicy gossip. 'Okay.'

'So, Byron brought home a girl the other night and well she's a bit of a screamer.'

'Tell him to get out of the relationship ASAP. She's obviously not the girl for him if in the honeymoon stage she's already screaming at him.'

Kayleigh laughed. 'She's not screaming at him, more screaming with him. You know, like in the bedroom.'

I snorted as I chuckled. 'Oh, go Byron!'

'So, do you think I can ask him to tell her to keep it down? I don't want to listen to my flat mate getting it on.'

'Maybe he could play some Barry White music to drown out the squeals of ecstasy.'

'Yeah, maybe not. That would make it even more filthy.'

'You could wear earplugs to block the noise.'

'Nope. Not doing that either,' Kayleigh replied.

'Well then you might have to talk to him and just

let him know it makes you feel uncomfortable. At least if you acknowledge it, he can tell her.'

'How embarrassing! How do I work it into conversation? Do I just say, "hey we are out of milk and by the way, I feel awkward when your girlfriend squeals the house down when she has an orgasm" or something like that?'

I snorted again. 'Yep, something like that.'

Kayleigh rolled her eyes and laughed. 'It's hard when you don't have a boyfriend and then you have to listen to other people getting hot and heavy. You don't know how lucky you are to live alone.'

I looked around the room and although it was cramped, it was the first time I felt grateful for my little place, which had suddenly started to feel like a home over the past few days. Who knew what I needed in my life was to adopt a little kitten and to share a wine with my best friend?

FALLING

Chris sat opposite my desk and fiddled nervously with his coat. This was the first time he had come to my office to get his dreams deciphered.

'How are you Chris?' I asked as I straightened my notepad. Marmie was curled in a ball under my desk. Her eyes had opened in the last few days and she was starting to sniff at smells. I felt like a mother, taking pride in all her little milestones.

Holding his hand up to stop me, Chris sneezed loudly. 'Sorry about that. My allergies are really playing up at the moment.' He sniffed and rubbed his eyes. 'I don't know if it's hay fever, or if I passed a cat on my way here, but my eyes are itchy, and my nose is blocked.'

I nodded sympathetically, making a mental note that I should probably not be bringing Marmalade to work. I just hoped she would remain asleep, so I wasn't caught out in the middle of the appointment.

'So, Chris, what dream would you like analysed?'

'Is this confidential? What I say here doesn't leave the room?'

'Yes, of course,' I answered, although there was no code of ethics for dream translation. I puffed out my chest, for the first time in my career feeling like a psychologist.

'Well, I had a dream that I was wearing this stunning gown and beautiful shoes. I felt like Cinderella at the ball. I was walking alongside this really handsome guy and then I tripped and fell over and he was laughing at me. I felt humiliated and when I woke up, I wondered why I was wearing a dress. I'm not gay you know. I felt so embarrassed by the dream and it's made me question if I'm secretly a cross dresser.'

'Chris, a dream of falling is an indication of insecurity or anxiety. Alongside that, a dream of cross-dressing doesn't make you gay or trans. It symbolizes a need for change. The man laughing at you just reinforces your insecurity because you want validation from this man, but instead you feel humiliated. I think you are aware of the fact that you suffer from anxiety that is inhibiting your life and you want to change that. Does that make sense?'

'Yes. I want to go for a promotion at work, but I'm paranoid that they will laugh at me applying, but I do honestly believe I can do the job better than the other candidates. My wife always tells me to have faith in myself.'

'Well I think your wife probably knows you really well and if she thinks you're capable, then maybe you should listen to her. Put yourself out there, ignore the anxiety, because I can guarantee, every single person going for that job will feel anxious about applying. You are one hundred percent guaranteed to fail to get the job if you don't apply, so your odds are significantly higher if you just believe in yourself and give it a go.'

Chris sneezed loudly again. 'Excuse me – damn allergies.'

'It's fine,' I replied, whilst silently praying that Marmie would remain asleep.

'I'm so relieved my dream wasn't about being gay. I've been so worried about it that I haven't told my wife about my dream or about coming to see you. I didn't know what I'd do if you told me I had to come out of the closet, because I've never felt any inclinations towards men.'

'I'm glad I can put your mind at ease. You just need to embrace your inner beauty and strengths and put your insecurities aside. I think you will be surprised by how it will positively affect your life.'

'Thank you so much Maggie. I appreciate your advice and feedback.'

'Good luck Chris,' I said, ushering him to the door. I had enough time between appointments that I could take Marmalade home and barricade her in the kitchen and get back to work for my next client. I looked out the window to check that Chris had left the building before picking up Marmie.

I jogged down the stairs holding Lady Marmalade in a box. With only a few steps left to walk, I noticed a man I'd never seen before entering the building. He was tall, broad shouldered and had dark wavy hair. I was so distracted by him that I slipped and missed the next step. In a blur I fell heavily and bumped my way down the stairs. In the frenzy, I'd held the box containing Marmalade up high, in an attempt to keep her safe. Thankfully the gorgeous stranger grabbed the box containing Marmalade who was boisterously crying after being jostled around unceremoniously.

'Are you okay cutie?' he asked in a sweet, gentle voice.

Although I had always complained about the extra junk in my trunk, it seemed there was barely enough padding to have protected me. The bruising on my buttocks and back would take longer to form than my already heavily bruised ego.

'I'm fine thanks. I'm so clumsy, it seems I missed a step and then…' I looked up to find the stranger staring at me with a quizzical expression. It was then I realized he had been gently talking to Marmalade. If only the earth could have swallowed me up at that moment!

I stood up straight. 'Umm, thanks for saving my kitten.'

'Oh no problem,' he replied before handing the box back to me.

I tucked the box under my arm and limped away with my kitten unharmed, unlike my dignity.

When I got to my car, I sat gingerly in the driver's seat and took a deep breath. My hands were still shaking slightly from the shock. I then did what I always do in the case of an emergency – I called Kayleigh.

'I have good news and bad news,' I started the conversation.

'Start with the good news,' Kayleigh replied jovially.

'Today I met the most gorgeous man I think I've ever seen.'

'Where did you meet said man, and when do I get to meet him?'

'He was in my office building. He was a nine and a half out of ten, and I'm not exaggerating. I didn't formally introduce myself, but he did talk briefly with Marmalade.'

'So, what's the bad news?' Kayleigh asked.

'Well I literally fell down the stairs in front of him and I may or may not have broken my back.' I half sobbed and half laughed.

'Are you serious? Are you okay?' Kayleigh asked with concern.

'I'll be okay. If I'd been a skinny chic, I would totally be in a wheelchair now with a broken hip. At least there's a silver lining to being a chunky mama.'

'Maggie, do you need to get an x-ray or anything? I can leave work and take you to the doctor if you want.'

'Thanks Kayleigh, you're such a good friend. I just needed to tell someone about my life and death experience today. I feel better already. Anyway, I have to rush back to work for another appointment.'

'Okay, well let me know if you need me. Take care lovely,' Kayleigh said before hanging up.

After dropping Marmalade home and creating a makeshift barricade to keep her in the kitchen, I returned to work. It was then I noticed a sign in the foyer of my office building that 'Zenith Model Management' had moved into the suite on the floor above mine. The mystery man was obviously a model and with my fingers crossed I hoped we would cross paths again one day. I also secretly hoped he suffered from amnesia so he wouldn't remember me bouncing down the stairs in front of him.

I was limping to my side of the desk when my next client entered.

'Hello, I'm Maggie,' I said, shaking hands.

As my new client Clara shook hands, bangles every shade of the rainbow jangled on her arm. 'Nice to meet you. I'm Clara.'

I hobbled to my seat and tentatively sat down. 'Do you want to tell me a bit about yourself, or just jump right into your dream?'

'I might just jump into the dream if that's okay.'

I nodded and took out my notepad and pen.

'I have a recurring dream, or maybe it is a nightmare, I'm not really sure. Anyway, in the dream there is a person chasing me that I can't see, but I know they are after me. I try to scream but there is no sound coming out. I have no voice whatsoever. The other night I woke up screaming. It really terrified my girlfriend who thought someone was attacking me.'

'Well Clara, being chased normally signifies that you are avoiding a person or a situation. Losing your voice is linked to feeling like your thoughts and opinions are not being heard. Does this resonate with you in your work or home life?'

Clara began to cry. 'My girlfriend Lana wants to introduce me to her family, but I haven't even come out to my family. My parents think Lana and I are just flat mates. I feel pressured to tell my parents that I'm gay, but I don't think they will accept it. On several occasions over the past few years I've started to broach the subject of the rights of gays and my dad always talks over me and says it's an abomination. I'm really worried that they will disown me. Lana keeps telling me I just have to bite the bullet and that regardless of their views, she will be there for me. At the moment I know my family loves me and I'm not sure I could cope with their rejection.'

'Clara, it's not my place to tell you what you should or shouldn't do, but it seems your subconscious is telling you that you are avoiding something that you need to deal with. Otherwise, you wouldn't have had that dream.'

'I know, but I just can't bring myself to do it. I've been in the closet my whole life; I can't imagine the reaction from my family if I outed myself.'

'Do you think you have more peace not being true to yourself?' I asked, my psychology degree getting put to some use.

'Probably not and I also worry that if I don't come out soon, then I might drive away Lana. She's asked me if I'm ashamed of her, which is crazy. I love her so much. But I also love my parents and I know they will be so disappointed in me.'

'It might take them some time to come to terms with it, but if they love you for who they think you are, let them love the real you. You don't have to be ashamed of who you are.'

'You're right. I am sick of living a lie. I know they adore Lana because they always say she is such a nice girl. My dad does grumble about her not being very ladylike having short hair, but he is traditional like that. You know what, it is time I put my big girl pants on and take control of my life. Thank you for giving me clarity.'

'Your subconscious is what gave you clarity and I'm just here to translate what it's telling you.'

Clara walked around the desk and wrapped me in a bear hug. I was torn between feeling humbled that I had made a difference and fainting with the pain of her arms squeezing the tender areas on my back.

Clara released me. 'Thank you so much Maggie.'

'It's my pleasure. Good luck with everything.'

With the final appointment of the day over, I packed up and headed home to soak in the bath. With all the talking I'd done that day, my voice was getting hoarse. Hopefully a bath would clear my head and ease my aching muscles.

As I stripped bare, I turned to look at my rear reflection in the mirror. I had purple welts evenly spaced down my back from my earlier fall.

Marmalade was in a box in the corner of the bathroom and I wondered what she made of me with my purple patches.

I eased myself into the bath, the water feeling simultaneously soothing and comforting.

I lay back and contemplated my clients over the last few days. This work was strangely satisfying, particularly seeing Clara take charge of her life today. It was an odd coincidence that Daisy had come to see me about her dream of a cat being rejected on the day I found Marmalade. Actually, come to think of it, it was also odd that Chris had discussed a dream about tripping and then I had fallen down the stairs earlier today. Surely, I wasn't re-enacting my client's dreams subconsciously. I tried to recall the dreams that I analysed at the radio station. One was flying, and the other was wrestling a snake. Thankfully they hadn't materialized.

My mind wandered back to Marmie. 'Hello gorgeous girl,' I called out to her, but it came out barely as a whisper. I cleared my throat and tried again. 'Marmie.' Again, my voice was barely audible. Great. I worked in a job that relied on me telling people what their dreams meant. How on earth could I do that when I couldn't talk?

My phone rang, startling me. I eased myself out of the bath and wrapped a towel around me.

'Hello,' I said, my voice reverberating in the hard-tiled bathroom.

'Hiya Maggie, I'm just ringing to see how you're feeling?' Kayleigh asked brightly.

'I'm okay,' I croaked hoarsely.

'What's up with your voice? Did you break your voice box in the fall too?'

'I've mysteriously lost my voice this afternoon.'

'Is your throat sore?' Kayleigh asked.

'No. It's fine. I just don't seem to have a voice,' I whispered.

'That's weird. It's like the universe has it out for you today,' Kayleigh joked.

'Kayleigh, tell me if this sounds like madness or just strange coincidences. I've seen three clients at my work this week that have shared their dreams with me. The first one had a dream of a cat and then I found Marmie. Before my fall today, my client had told me about a dream where he had tripped over and then my last client today had a dream where she was screaming and no sound was coming out and now I've lost my voice.'

'That is some freaky shit. I've got goose bumps on my arms.'

'So, do you think there is something to it? Do you think I'm subconsciously reenacting their dreams in my life?'

'I can't see how you have the ability to lose your voice. I guess they are coincidences. I mean, you are pretty clumsy, and a handsome man distracted you when you had your fall. Marmalade was just meant to come into your life. She is so lucky you rescued her.'

'I guess you're right. Maybe I hit my head when I fell and I'm not thinking very logically tonight.'

'Do you feel concussed? Perhaps I should take you to a doctor.'

'No, I'm fine, just an overactive imagination. I'm going to have an early night and hopefully I'll feel better in the morning.'

'Okay, well, I hope you feel better soon.'

'Thanks,' I croaked.

NIGHTMARE

The following morning, I awoke and my voice was barely audible. I was exhausted, as the aching in my back had woken me several times throughout the night. I looked at my schedule for the day. Thankfully I only had one appointment early in the morning. As much as I loved running my own business, the downside was there was no one I could delegate to. I resolved to just attend that one appointment, then call it a day and come home to rest.

I always took the long way from the car park towards my office to avoid walking past Jason's shop. I didn't want to look in and spy him working on fixing a computer, or worse, see his ex-ex strutting around the shop. There is only so much a girl's inferiority complex can take.

That morning, feeling sleep deprived and with an aching body, I couldn't care less if I walked past Jason. I just wanted to take the shortest route to work. I had a plan to studiously look at my phone while I walked past his shop, so I didn't have to see Jason or what's-her-name. I'm not being facetious. I really have no idea what her name is, and I doubt Jason does either.

Anyway, I was walking towards the door to the office foyer when a voice called out, 'You had better be careful being on your phone while you walk. You don't want to trip over.'

I was going to give the smart arse a talking to. After all, no one had the right to tell me what to do. I slowly raised my gaze and saw the gorgeous man from the day before holding the door open for me. He was grinning and had the most adorable dimple in his cheek. My mouth was already forming the letter F, which I then quickly transformed into 'fank you.' As if it wasn't bad enough that he thought I was a clumsy cow, I was humiliated that I now sounded like I also had a speech impediment.

'Are you okay? That was quite a tumble yesterday. Where's your cat?'

'I've left the cat at home today,' I replied hoarsely as I hobbled towards the stairs.

'I wish I could take a pet to work,' he said smiling. His brilliantly straight, bright white teeth dazed me. 'I'm Levi, by the way.'

'Like the jeans?' I asked.

He rolled his eyes. 'The jeans are like me,' he replied laughing.

'I'm Maggie. I'm the Dream Analyst on level one.'

'What a cool job! I'll have to get you to analyse my dreams one day.'

I limped up the stairs. 'Well, I'll see you around Levi,' I said as I unlocked my office door.

'Okay,' he said as he climbed the stairs towards his office on the floor above.

Well, at least the hot guy in the building now had a name. It would give me something to go by when I ultimately wanted to stalk him on his social media, which being realistic, I knew would be as soon as my appointment was finished. In fact, I think maybe I missed my calling in life. I would have made an awesome private investigator. Stalking is my favourite hobby - the trail of digital matter people leave out like breadcrumbs is tantalizing.

Judy was an elderly lady, and by elderly I mean, over fifty. She had mousy brown hair with a streak of grey in the front. The previous time Judy had seen me, she had left with a huge smile on her face. I didn't recall the dream, but I did remember her reaction to my interpretation of it.

'Hi Maggie,' Judy said as she sat down.

'How are you?' I asked, my voice barely a whisper.

'I'm good. By the sounds of it, I'm better than you. Are you unwell?'

'I've lost my voice. I don't have a cold or sore throat. Please just excuse my voice.'

'No problems. I meant to tell you that I've been seeing a psychologist for my anxiety and phobias,' she replied.

I really should have looked up notes in her case file so I could recall what she was talking about.

'That's good. Is it helping?' I asked.

'I think so, however there is one phobia that is really bothering me, and I've been dreaming about it. In my dream, I'm in a dark room, full of spiders. They are crawling all over me and although I try to squash them, more come at me.' I could see Judy's revulsion as she recalled the dream.

I shuddered. I have my own issues with spiders

so I could totally relate to her fear.

'Well, spiders can relate to feeling like you are being manipulated and being drawn into someone's web. They can also relate to feeling isolated and wanting to be let back into an inner circle of friends. Do either of these mean anything to you?'

'My husband Keith doesn't like me going out with my girlfriends. He doesn't understand why I need friends beyond him. He doesn't have any male friends he meets up with, so he is always grumpy if I arrange to have coffee or dinner with my girlfriends. It makes me feel sick with anxiety to even raise the subject with him.'

'Do you feel that you are being rejected by your friends because of his controlling ways?'

'They tell me that I should ignore him, but sometimes I just don't think it is worth the hassle of having him angry at me, to have a quick coffee with them. I know that if I keep declining their invitations that they will just stop including me, which also makes me feel sick with anxiety.'

'It sounds to me like you are feeling manipulated by Keith. Did you know that women generally speak three times as much as men? Maybe you could have a calm talk with Keith and explain that while his company is very important to you, that you need social interaction with other people too. It's no wonder you feel anxious about going out to see your friends if you feel like you are starting a fight to do so.'

Judy was winding her hair around and around her finger. I noticed the tip of her finger was turning purple.

'I don't know how he would take that,' Judy said, winding her hair more furiously.

'It sounds to me that maybe Keith is a bit insecure. Maybe you could suggest a dinner party with your friends and their partners. That way Keith has the opportunity to get to know your friends better, he can meet their husbands and forge new friendships with them, and you don't have to choose who to spend your time with.'

'I hadn't thought of that. It might be worth trying.' Judy released her hair and with relief, I saw the colour of her fingertip resume a normal skin tone. I had been worried she might amputate her finger had she wound the hair any tighter.

'It's really interesting what your inner subconscious is trying to tell you. Once you know the significance of a dream, it gives you a starting point to deal with the issue.'

'I'm so glad to be able to see you. I have to book another appointment for next month, and also, my niece wants your business card so she and some of her friends can come. She listens to you on the radio and she is totally fascinated by what you do.'

'I'd love to meet her and hopefully give her clarity like I've been able to give to you.' I handed over a wad of business cards. It gave me such satisfaction to be building my business and to have return clients.

'Let's just hope you have cured me of dreaming about spiders. I'd rather dream about Chris Hemsworth,' Judy said as she grinned and winked.

I laughed. What a little minx! That was the last comment I expected to hear from her. I just hope poor old Keith doesn't find out that Judy has a soft spot for Chris Hemsworth, otherwise he might ban her from watching his movies.

When I opened my front door, Marmie meowed loudly from the kitchen, greeting me. She was obviously bored and craving some company. I reached down and scooped her into my arms. She instantly burrowed her head into the crook of my neck and began purring loudly. I'd had no idea how lovely it was to find a creature to adore you like this. I playfully ruffled the fur between her ears.

Within a minute Marmie had grown weary of being restrained. I put her down and set about making myself a cup of tea to ease my hoarse throat. I climbed over the barrier cordoning off the kitchen from the rest of my home. I knew my days of keeping Marmie contained in the kitchen were limited. Now that she was able to walk around, I was thrilled when I looked over at her kitty litter tray and saw the evidence that she had been using it. Even more thrilling was the fact that there were no puddles that I could see on the floor. Who knew it was humanly possible for someone to be so excited by seeing signs of their cat's defecation?

I sat on the lounge with my steaming hot Earl Grey tea in hand. Marmie rubbed herself up against my shins, winding in a figure eight around my legs. As I sipped the tea, I mentally reviewed today's case. If there was any chance my clients were transferring their dreams to me, I was terrified that I might now encounter spiders. I scanned the room. There was a very filmy spider's web up high on the cornice, but there was a fair chance that had been there since before I moved in. I laughed aloud at my absurd thought. I was an intelligent, educated woman, who wasn't normally prone to ridiculous fantasies.

I pushed aside my unease and instead set to what I do best. I opened my laptop and began firstly by stalking Levi. It didn't take too long to find him, and his Instagram feed was full of photos of him barely dressed, lounging by pools or with a towel casually flung over his shoulder. I thought he was gorgeous in real life, but the photos he had shared were drool worthy. His bio said that he was a booking agent at Zenith Model Agency, but clearly, he also modeled as his feed was like a spread for bachelor of the year. I made a specific note that he hadn't put any relationship status on his bio, so it appeared not only was he single, but he was ready to mingle.

I pulled up the opening hours of the gym where I had a membership. Maybe Levi would consider dating me if I looked trim, taut and terrific. Although the gym was open, I decided it was best to let my body rest at the moment. Not only was I stiff and sore from my fall but I must be rundown, given the fact that I had practically lost my voice. I vowed that as soon as I was fully healthy, I would start my new exercise regime.

While I had my computer open, I quickly stalked Jason and what's-her-name. Not that I longed to rekindle anything with Jason, I just hoped to find evidence that maybe there might be some trouble in paradise. I'm a big believer in karma and so I knew at some point things would come crashing down for Jason and I wanted a front-row seat to watch when it did. Okay, I know that makes me sound like a psycho, but it's not like I was doing anything to sabotage their relationship. I just had a vested interest. I really hoped Jason one day would be blindsided and left hurt and wounded, just as he had rejected me.

It appeared that Kween Rosy was busy sightseeing in Sydney. All her photos were of her in front of the Harbour Bridge or Opera House. Given the photos were taken mid week, I wondered whether she had found a job or was just living the life of a lady of leisure.

I was pulled from my reverie as I heard my neighbour drag their wheelie bin out to the curb. I'd forgotten it was bin collection night. I vowed tonight, under the cover of darkness, to do some snooping in my neighbours' bins to see if I could find any evidence of purple bin liners. The mystery of the cat dumper was still unsolved, and I wanted justice for Marmie.

After watching back-to-back episodes of Sex in the City, I turned off the television and pulled the curtains aside to peek outside. Most houses were in darkness. It was time to do some detective work. I scooped up my rubbish and quietly tiptoed, as best I could in UGG boots, out to my garbage bin. Wanting to be stealthy, I decided to delay rolling my bin to the curb. I quietly skulked along the street, using the torch in my phone to peer into my neighbours' bins. With each lid I lifted I worried that a lurking spider might attack me, but with relief my arachnid fears were not made into reality. Each bin had a distinct waft of rotting food that made me want to gag, but none used purple bin liners. As I reached the end of my street, a spotlight landed on me. A man I've never met yelled out from his front porch, 'What are you doing?'

Like a fugitive I began to race away from the scene. I'd read somewhere that it was best to zigzag when you ran to avoid being caught, or was it being shot, I couldn't remember. I took a few steps one wasy, and then quickly changed direction. The torchlight followed me, obviously proving the zigzag theory incorrect for running and making me look a drunken sprinter. I turned around to stare at the source and was blinded by the light. The next step I took was off the edge of the gutter, rolling my ankle badly. I lay whimpering on the side of the road. The torchlight got bigger and brighter until a large man stood over the top of me.

'Are you okay?' he asked.

'Yep, I'm fine,' I squeaked, trying to hold back tears.

'What are you doing out here and why were you looking through my rubbish?'

I looked up and saw that he wore a look of pure confusion. He pushed his dark curly hair off his face, and I got my first real look at him. Apart from floating black spots, as a result of looking directly into a flashlight, he appeared to be quite attractive. Not a Levi level of gorgeousness, but a swipe right on Tinder type of handsome.

'Someone dumped a newborn kitten in my bin a few weeks ago. I figured that person probably lives locally, and I wanted to find out who it was. So, I wasn't targeting your bin specifically. I was just hunting for the scumbag that had done it.'

'So, were you looking for cat food tins and kitty litter? There are a lot of people on this street with cats,' he said, looking amused at my novice detective work.

'No. The kitten was disposed of in a purple bin liner. I was looking to see who uses those.'

'Did you find any purple bin liners in the street?' he asked.

'I only got as far as your place, before you

frightened me off. I haven't checked out the other side of the street. And now, I'm not really sure if I can even walk.'

'Here, give me your hand.' He took my hand in his and pulled me up to a standing position.

I couldn't weight bare, so I just stood holding the stranger's hand, taking deep breaths that may or may not have sounded like sobs.

'I'm Sam, by the way,' he said, pumping the hand he held up and down in a handshake.

'I'm Maggie,' I replied awkwardly.

'So Maggie, where do you live? I'll help you back to your house.'

I pointed at the villa. '35a is my current abode,' I said, hoping to sound jovial, although my voice sounded a bit odd to my ears due to the raspiness as well as clenching my teeth to deal with the excruciating pain in my ankle.

Sam wrapped his arm around my waist and placed my arm over his shoulder to support me to limp to my house. Suddenly my focus was less on the pain in my ankle and more on my muffin top spilling over the waistband of my tracksuit pants. I sucked in, trying to make the said bulge disappear but it stubbornly refused to move.

As I opened the door, Marmie rushed to see who was visiting. Sam scooped her up with his free arm to stop me from tripping on her and he then eased me onto the lounge.

'I guess this is the kitten you are out to get justice for,' Sam said, tickling Marmalade behind the ears. She would never make a guard cat; she was purring loudly from the attention.

'Yes. Your new best friend there is Lady Marmalade.'

'Hello little lady. Aren't you sweet?'

'Well thanks for coming to my rescue,' I said, trying to hint for him to leave.

'Have you got any ice? You really need to elevate your ankle and ice it for the best recovery.'

Sam walked towards the fridge and then yanked open the freezer door. I cringed inside. Normal people have a freezer full of frozen meals and vegetables. I had three half eaten tubs of ice cream, because you never know what flavour you will feel like eating, and a bottle of vodka. If I could have read his mind, I just knew he would have been thinking: this is how she got the muffin top. Thankfully he located the lone ice-tray and emptied the contents into a tea towel for me to rest on my ankle. I slipped my UGG boot off and looked at my swollen joint. I put it up next to my other ankle to compare, but then realised I actually have cankles. They both looked puffy, although my left one looked slightly puffier. I gingerly lay the makeshift icepack on my injury.

'Do you have any painkillers here you can take?'

I kept them in the bathroom but recalling that I'd left my pyjamas and dirty underwear on the floor, I didn't want him to go in there.

'No, but I'll be fine. Thank you for coming to my rescue.' I smiled shyly at Sam. 'Sorry I was snooping around in your bin.'

'No problems. In fact, now that I've met Lady Marmalade, I will have to take up your crusade to find the cat dumper. On my way home, I'll check out the bins on the other side of the street. Is there anything else I can do for you before I go?' he asked.

My heart swooned. Who knew there were decent guys still left in the world? 'If you don't mind, would you wheel my bin out to the street? I haven't put my own bin out yet.'

'Sure, I'll do that. Well if I find the culprit, I'll let you know. Take care.'

'Thanks Sam. By the way, it's nice to meet you.'

Sam laughed. 'Yeah, you too.'

I hopped to the window and peeked through the crack in the curtains. Sam, true to his word, was strolling down the far side of the street from one bin to another to search for evidence.

I managed to limp to the bathroom to take some painkillers and then flopped into bed. Exhausted from the day and wanting to rest my leg I turned out the light and drifted off to sleep.

In my dream, Levi was gently kissing my neck, making his way up towards my ear. He stopped and his smoldering eyes looked deep into my soul. He smiled and the dimple on his cheek only enhanced his picture-perfect face. 'You're so amazing,' he whispered into my ear. My resolve to hold out on him faltered. What was a woman supposed to do when a sex demigod threw himself at her? His feather light kisses continued across my cheek. I moaned with pure desire. He then continued until he tried to crawl inside my nose.

My eyes opened wide, and I sat bolt upright, feeling something wriggling near my nose. A large, hairy spider was burrowing into my nostril. I squealed as I flung it across the room and then turned on my bedside lamp. The gargantuan huntsman spider was starting to run across the carpet towards me, so without a second thought I threw the Agatha Christie novel that was sitting on my bedside table on top of it. I then hopped over and with my sore foot, pressed as hard as I dared to ensure the spider had been eradicated. I tentatively pulled up *Death on the Nile* and looked underneath to find the spider well and truly squashed. A small squirt of its guts were smeared across the cover of the book, that from that day forward would be known to me as *Death on the Shag Pile*.

My heart was racing as I hopped back to bed. The dream of Levi had been exhilarating, but finding a spider trying to make a nest in my nose was a whole new level of terror to anything I had experienced before. Damn bloody Judy telling me a dream about spiders today. This was beyond a coincidence. I was fully convinced that my client's dreams were turning into my reality. If only I could have a client tell me a dream about Levi and me kissing, I'd be more than happy to have that dream come true.

My throbbing ankle woke me from my restless sleep. I pulled back the doona to survey the damage.

The site of my injury was the shade fashion bloggers may refer to as aubergine – purply/blue and shiny from the skin being stretched across the swollen joint. As I lowered my foot to the floor, the throbbing intensified. I swear I could almost see it beating like a sub-woofer playing rap music. I hopped as far as the bathroom, taking deep breaths between swearing at myself. I hastily swallowed some painkillers and then hopped back to bed.

A fine sweat had broken out all over my body due to the exertion of hopping with a nine out of ten pain rating. The positive thing was that the pain in my ankle had taken my attention away from the bruises on my back. I placed my foot on a pillow and reached for my phone. My first priority was to cancel my appointments for the day, which given my epiphany that their dreams were becoming my reality, was more than I would have been able to face that day.

I then called Kayleigh. 'Hey Kayls, it's me,' I said in a voice dull enough to convey my current condition.

'Hey Maggie. Are you okay? You sound a bit flat.'

'I'm a walking train wreck. Last night I was running away from my neighbour and I rolled my ankle. It's really sore and really swollen.'

'Why were you running away from your neighbour?'

'He caught me snooping in his bin.'

Kayleigh laughed. 'Why were you snooping in his bin?'

'I was checking the contents of all my neighbours' bins to see who uses purple bin liners. I'm going to catch the kitten dumper if it's the last thing I do.'

'Oh, I see. So, I gather you didn't catch the culprit.'

'No but I did meet my neighbour. Once I rolled my ankle, he was actually really sweet and helped my back to my home.'

'He sounds nice. Maybe when you're feeling better, you could catch up with him to thank him for his assistance.'

'Hmm, maybe. Listen Kayls, I know you saw a good physiotherapist when you hurt your back in that surfing accident. I think I need to see someone and to get some crutches to get around.'

'Yeah, he was located next to the gym. I can't remember his name but it's something religious, I think. He is cute and seemed really nice. Anyway, the place is called Good Sports Physio. I can call and make an appointment for you and then I'll come pick you up and take you if you like.'

'You are the best. Thank you, Kayleigh. I don't know how I can repay you.'

'When you're better, you can take me out for a mojito.'

Only minutes after hanging up, I received a text from Kayleigh confirming she had got an appointment for me at 12.30pm.

Twenty minutes before the appointment, Kayleigh arrived on the doorstep with flowers and a frozen meal. She really was a godsend.

By the time I hobbled into the physio, I was spent, and by the looks of it, Kayleigh was too. Her fitness was much better than mine, but having a semi-dead weight leaning on her as we made our way to the physio was a full-on workout for her. As I sat in the waiting room, I peered out the window to a sign the gym had placed outside the door. I had finally reached a point of realisation that it was no good just having a membership. The time had come to start using it. Well, the time hadn't actually come right now as I couldn't even walk, but once I was mobile again the time would be right.

Kayleigh told the receptionist I was there to see Samson Telavatu and then returned to sit next to me.

'Maggie McIntyre,' a male voice called out.

I looked up and locked eyes with Sam. His eyes twinkled as a grin spread across his face. 'Well, if it isn't the cat burglar! Are you stalking me?'

I laughed feebly as I felt heat flush across my cheeks. What were the chances that my neighbour was the physio? 'Kayleigh, Sam is my neighbour who helped me last night.'

'Wow, isn't it a small world?' Kayleigh replied as she helped me stand and supported me as I limped towards the treatment room. 'He is cute, isn't he?' she whispered, way too loudly for my liking.

Sam helped me up onto the treatment bed and gently placed my leg on a pillow.

'I'll wait outside.' Kayleigh winked at me as she left the room. The blush that I knew was making me look like a tomato was not likely to subside with her acting like that.

'It was quite a tumble you took last night,' Sam

said as he started to feel my foot. 'I just want to check for any broken bones.' He gingerly rotated the foot and poked and prodded. It was painful but not curl up in the foetal position type pain. 'I think you've sprained your ankle and will need rest for a few days. What do you do for a job?'

'I'm a dream analyst,' I replied, searching his face for signs of skepticism.

'Cool, sounds like a dream job.' He thought this pun was hilarious.

I rolled my eyes and shook my head, although I couldn't help but laugh at his goofiness, even if I had heard that joke every time I spoke about work with my dad for the past four years.

'You are going to need crutches. I'll just grab them for you.'

He disappeared for a moment and I took a look around the room. There was a photo of Sam in a blue jersey that hugged his bulky chest, with a rugby ball tucked under his arm.

When he returned, he set the grips on the crutches to the level I needed.

'So, you play football?' I asked, pointing to the photo.

'Not anymore. I used to play for the Waratahs but had a knee reconstruction back in 2012, so now I just help people heal from their injuries.'

I didn't know what the Waratahs was, but he looked a little bit smug when he said it, so I figured it was something to be proud of. I mentally logged the name of the team so I could do some stalking of Sam.

'Maggie, you need to elevate the leg and take painkillers every four hours for the next few days. Do you need a doctor's certificate to miss work?'

'No, it's okay. I run my own business.'

'Oh, I almost forgot, I looked in all the bins on the other side of the road and there was no sign of any purple bags. So, I guess it is back to square one.'

'Thanks for taking over my detective work and thanks for helping me last night. You didn't tell me that you were a physio.'

'I didn't want you to think I was trying to be an ambulance chaser. Plus, I gave you the same advice as I would have if you were my patient.'

I nodded and stood to wedge the crutches under my arms. As a child I always wanted to have crutches, but within a few moments, the joy I had expected to feel evaporated as I came to realise they were cumbersome and uncomfortable.

'Good luck. Once the swelling goes down, if you have any problems with mobility you can call me.' He scribbled his mobile number on his business card. 'I might even be convinced to offer you a home visit as it would be the neighbourly thing to do.'

'Thanks Sam,' I said trying to co-ordinate walking with crutches.

On the way home, I was chatting with Kayleigh in the car.

'I didn't tell you about the spider climbing up my nose last night.'

Kayleigh sniggered. 'That would only ever happen to you.'

'You know how the other day I was telling you about the strange coincidences between my client's dreams and what was happening to me? Well yesterday I had a lady tell me her dream about a spider. All day I was paranoid that I was going to see a spider. I was literally checking out the cornices in the lounge room to see if I could see a daddy long legs spider or something lame like that.

Anyway, I was having a dream that Levi, the beautiful model that works in my building, was kissing up my neck and across my cheek. Actually, now that I think about it, I think it was actually the spider crawling on me.' I shivered involuntarily. 'I woke up when the spider was trying to climb up my nostril.'

Kayleigh chuckled.

'I flicked that sucker across the room but then it was running towards me as if it didn't like getting evicted from its new home. I finally managed to squash it under a book. It was the biggest, hairiest huntsman spider you have ever seen. I'm not sure I will ever be able to get a good night's sleep again.'

'Oh well, at least it is dead now, so you don't have to worry about it being a squatter in your nose anymore.' At this point Kayleigh snorted as she laughed and I swear I could see tears pooling in her eyes, ready to run down her face in her state of merriment.

'My point is that my life is being hijacked by my client's dreams. What if someone comes and tells me a dream where they are killed in a fire or they drown in a bathtub? I can't run the risk of that happening.'

Kayleigh had the decency to stop laughing and

even wiped the tears from her cheeks. 'Oh hun, that's not going to happen. You can't live in fear of your client's dreams. There is the chance that one of them will dream of you winning the lottery or getting a huge inheritance from a long-lost aunt.'

'I want to test this theory before I take any more clients. It appears that it's only the dreams that I analyse in my office that come true. The ones on the radio and for the magazine aren't affecting me. What if you come and tell me you had a dream about kissing Levi? I could then see if it would lead to Levi and I kissing. I'd be more than willing for that to come true.'

'Sure. There's no harm in trying, although for the record I do think they have all just been strange coincidences. I don't believe anyone can be responsible for making things happen in your life.'

'Fine. I'll prove it. Let's swing by my work and we can start the strictly scientific experiment that I shall call Levi Smoochathon 1.0.'

DREAM MAN

Trying to use crutches whilst climbing the stairs seemed an almost impossible feat. I tried first to place my crutches on the ground and swing my foot up to the first step, but then swung back in a full arc. I grabbed the balustrade to help support me but my crutch on that side just slipped to the floor. Eventually, Kayleigh grabbed the discarded crutch, and I hopped up one step at a time. I made a mental note to start my new gym regime with a step class.

By the time I reached the landing outside my office I was sweating profusely. I wiped the beads of perspiration off my top lip, just as Levi bounded down the stairs. My heart skipped a beat.

'Hi Levi,' I said, waving my crutch at him like a crazy woman.

'Oh, hi Maggie. What have you done to yourself now?'

'I've sprained my ankle,' I said leaning on my

crutch trying to make it look seductive.

Kayleigh coughed lightly. I'd totally forgotten she was there. 'Oh Levi, this is my friend Kayleigh.'

I'm sure I heard Kayleigh give a little sigh. 'Hi, it's nice to meet you.'

'Yeah, you too,' Levi said, flashing his megawatt smile. I wondered whether he had insurance to cover his smile, although I wasn't sure you could really put a price on such beauty.

'Hey Maggie, I wanted to ask you a favour. You seem really melodramatic.' I nodded, not sure if he was trying to compliment or offend me. 'And well, I want to sign up for an acting class, because I don't want to be modeling all my life. Would you be interested in joining with me? I'd prefer to have someone there that I know.'

I looked over Levi's shoulder to see Kayleigh nodding her head wildly, like a bobble-head figurine on the dashboard of a car four-wheel driving.

'Sounds like fun. When is it?' I had never contemplated acting, but maybe the universe thought this would be a good career move for me. It might be a way to move out of dream analysing.

'It starts tonight at 6.30pm,' he replied smiling.

'Tonight? As in today? As in a few hours?'

'Yep. I can drive since it seems you're probably not up to it.'

To be honest, I was really only up to lying in bed watching Netflix, but when you get asked out on a life changing adventure, what does a throbbing, swollen ankle matter?

'Great. I'll just get your number so I can text you my address.'

After I said farewell to Levi, with his phone number logged in my phone and deep in my memory, I turned to Kayleigh. She was doing a happy dance, or something to that effect.

'O.M.G. I can't believe you just got asked out by the most beautiful man alive.'

I squealed. 'I know. What were the chances?'

'I had no idea you were interested in acting.'

I laughed. 'Neither did I, but who am I to turn down the opportunity to get to know him better?'

'Now I really can't wait to see if I can make your kiss a reality. Sit down, I've got a saucy dream to tell you,' Kayleigh said winking.

I hobbled to my chair. 'Okay, let me have it.'

'Well,' Kayleigh said winking, 'I had a dream last night about Levi.' She stopped to wink again. 'In the dream we were walking down a beach, hand in hand and then he stopped.' She giggled and winked again. At this stage, I was worried she had developed a nervous tick in her left eye. 'His thumb stroked my cheek and then we kissed.' Wink, wink, wink. 'What do you think this means?'

'Well I think it means one of two things. One – you're obsessed by the gorgeousness of him, or two – he is a really good kisser. I sort of think both.'

'Now that I've met sexiness personified, I understand the obsession. If things don't work out for you two, then make sure you give him my phone number.'

I was nervous as I slowly shuffled my way into the drama class. It was being held in a small local theatre and the acting coach was on the stage. He dramatically clapped his hands together in order to get everyone's attention. I flopped into a fold up chair, just as he asked us all to join him on stage. I had to fish around for the crutch that had slid to the ground when I sat down and then with the speed of an exhausted sloth, I made my way to the stage. The stairs didn't have a handrail, so rather than try to go up the stairs with my crutches, I sat on my bottom and shuffled up one step after another. Who knew this being injured caper was such a great cardio workout?

The acting tutor was handing out scripts to all the able-bodied students. By the time I made it to the group he was out of printed scripts.

'We are starting today with a brief appropriation of Romeo and Juliet. You all have your roles highlighted. I want to see what talent you have and what we will need to work on over the course of this term.'

I raised my hand, trying to lodge my crutch between my elbow and rib. 'Excuse me, I didn't get a role.'

'That's fine darling, I kept the most pivotal role for you. You will be Juliet.'

I puffed up my chest, ecstatic to have been assigned the lead role. 'Okay.'

'Everyone take your places. Cripple girl, you come lie here on the ground. Juliet has just been drugged and lays unconscious on the stage.'

My short-lived joy was extinguished. I was playing an unconscious character.

I lay down on the cold hard stage, crossing my legs to try to elevate my swollen ankle. I clasped my hands together over my abdomen.

'No, no, no. Handicap girl, you need to look like you've collapsed. You have no control of your muscles. I want to see your jaw slack and your eyes rolled back in your head. Romeo needs to believe you are dead.'

I relaxed my jaw, adding about four chins to my already double chin and arranged my body like a discarded doll.

'That's better. Now try not to breathe. No one wants to see your chest rising and falling. We, the audience, have to also think you are dead.'

I held my breath, but after five seconds I had to expel. I'd never make a free diver. I opted instead for micro-breaths to minimise my chest movement.

'This modern version of Romeo and Juliet is set in a disused warehouse where there are junkies sprawled around. Juliet's dad wants her to straighten up and marry a family friend, but she loves her drug dealer boyfriend Romeo.'

The actors around me read their lines and then I heard Levi. It was clear he was my Romeo and I couldn't think of a more romantic start to a relationship. In years to come we could tell our grandkids that on our first date we played Romeo and Juliet.

'Juliet, what's up? Why won't you speak to me? Are you ghosting me or are you just asleep? Did you shoot up with too much angel dust?'

The dialogue in the play was dreadful and Levi's acting was wooden and strained.

He knelt before me and I could smell the waft of garlic from the Italian meal he had eaten before picking me up. He lifted my limp hand to his cheek.

'Wake up Boo, wake up. Oh my God, can it really be that she is dead? The angel dust has finally taken her to heaven.' If I hadn't been playing dead, I would have rolled my eyes. Who wrote this shite?

Levi nestled my head in his lap, and I could feel a small rivulet of drool had dribbled out of my mouth. I just hoped the lighting was dim enough that he wouldn't notice. He lent down and pressed his mouth to my slack-jawed open mouth. This wasn't the way I had envisioned our first kiss, but it was a start.

'Cut. That's a wrap,' the acting coach said clapping campily.

I sat up and smiled at Levi. He was beaming with

pride. While I thought my performance was extremely convincing, I didn't have the heart to tell him that his acting kinda sucked. I only hoped that by the end of the course, he would have learned the tricks of the trade and would be a credible actor.

'That was a good start and I now have notes to work with. Next week we will start workshopping showing emotions and crying on demand. I want you all to go home and practice crying in front of the mirror.'

I bum-shuffled my way back over to the stage stairs and bounced my way down again before lodging the crutches back into position. At least now we were done, I could go home, pop some painkillers and play with Marmie.

'Thanks again for coming along with me,' Levi said smiling. 'I just knew you would be a natural.'

I smiled. I knew I had really nailed looking unconscious.

'How was I?' Levi asked.

I plastered a fake smile on my face. How could I be diplomatic about his dreadful acting?

'I couldn't see your acting on account of my being unconscious, but I think it is a good starting point.'

Levi grinned his megawatt smile and inside I shivered. He could just dazzle audiences with his beauty, and no one would notice his lame acting.

'Maggie, I was wondering if you would mind dropping by my friend's bar for a drink. It's opening night, and I said that I'd go. You don't mind, do you?'

I ignored the throbbing in my ankle; there wasn't a snowballs chance in hell that I wouldn't go for a drink with the most gorgeous human being alive. 'I'd love to.'

As we drove up to the bar, there was a queue lined up around the block. 'Oh, there's a huge queue. I'm not sure I can stand around for that long with my sore ankle.'

Levi looked at me quizzically. 'Huh?'

'I've got a sprained ankle. I didn't just accessorize with the crutches for fun.'

'Babe, we don't have to wait in line, my name's on the list.'

My breathing hitched. He just called me babe. Things were moving fast.

As Levi strutted towards the bouncer, I hobbled as fast as I could. The red velvet cord was moved to the side to allow the entrance of the beautiful one (and his disabled companion).

The interior of the bar was opulence incarnate. A large crystal chandelier hung above the entrance foyer and glass and mirrors highlighted the decadent decor. We were led towards a VIP area and slid into a black velvet padded booth. Levi draped his hand across the back of the cushion behind me. I felt like Cinderella at the ball. I'd never dreamed my life could be so glamorous.

'What would you like to drink?' asked a waitress, dressed in a figure hugging black unitard.

'Two champagnes, thanks,' Levi replied.

I leaned over to talk in Levi's ear. 'This place is incredible.'

'Yeah. It's cool,' he replied.

Our conversation was cut short when another ridiculously beautiful guy walked towards us. Levi stood and gave him a hearty bro hug.

'Congrats Ben. This place is awesome.'

'Thanks. It's such a relief that it is finally open. I'm really glad you could make it.'

I sat in the booth, feeling like a shag on a rock. I couldn't easily stand to greet Levi's friend and so I just smiled at him.

Ben lent over and whispered in Levi's ear. He laughed and then turned to me. 'Ben, this is my friend Maggie. We go to acting classes together.'

Ben nodded at me and I put my hand out to shake his, at the same time as he turned to talk to a passing waitress. My hand was just left hovering in limbo. I settled for a wave at a random stranger across the room and then put my hand back down to rest in my lap. If that wasn't the epitome of awkwardness, then I didn't know what was.

Levi walked to the other side of the booth and he slid in followed by Ben.

'I can't stay long,' Ben said, his eyes roaming around the room. It was only reasonable that his attention would be drawn by everything going on around him on his opening night.

'Your bar is stunning,' I yelled over the music that loudly thumped through the state-of-the-art sound system.

'Thanks,' he replied.

The waitress in the unitard returned with a bottle of Dom Perignon Champagne and three glasses. I looked at her, okay so maybe it actually classified as ogling. I couldn't imagine squeezing my body into a lycra onesie. There wasn't an ounce of fat on her lithe body. She smiled seductively at Levi and in that moment, I wanted to scratch out her immaculately wing-lined eyes. Levi didn't seem to notice her, which gave my heart a flutter. Okay, she could keep her eyes – for now.

Levi poured the champagne with a flourish. We all raised our glasses. 'To you,' Levi said smiling at Ben. We clinked glasses, and I sipped, savouring the tiny bubbles in the French champagne.

Wait until I told Kayleigh about my night. She wouldn't believe it. I pulled out my phone to take a few photos. The flash burst light out across the room and everyone within a ten metre radius turned to stare at me. 'My bad,' I said, hastily turning off the flash setting.

I leaned down to put my phone back into my handbag and noticed under the table, Ben's hand high in Levi's crotch. I sat up straight and looked at Levi. His head was thrown back as he laughed at Ben's comment.

'I really need to get home,' I said. My pride hurt more than my ankle.

Levi looked at Ben. 'You know if I didn't have a

shoot at 9am, I'd be here all night, but I need my beauty sleep. I'll leave my door open. Come by when you finish here.'

Ben winked at Levi. 'I'll see you then.'

I stood, forgetting about my injured ankle, and immediately saw stars. I wasn't entirely sure if it was from the throbbing pain or the humiliation that I had totally misread my relationship with Levi. My gaydar definitely required fine tuning.

'Nice to meet you Ben,' I said, but he had already turned and walked away.

In the car on the way home I turned towards Levi. 'So, you and Ben seem close.'

Levi nodded, 'Yeah, he's a good friend.'

'Just a friend?' I asked, trying to keep the whine out of my voice.

'Uh huh, friends with benefits.'

'Cool,' I replied. I didn't really know what more to say. 'You know I'm all for gay pride and all that.' As soon as the words were out of my mouth, I wanted to grab them and shove them back in.

'Okay,' Levi said nodding.

'I mean I voted for marriage equality. Not that I'm saying you two should marry, or maybe you should. The point is that at least now you can if you want to.' My verbal diarrhea kept flowing.

'Okay,' Levi replied.

'Look to be honest, I didn't realise before tonight that you were gay. But I want you to know that I support your choices.'

Levi laughed. 'Honey, you didn't think someone with bone structure like mine could actually be straight, did you?'

I laughed as if it was the most ludicrous thing in the world. 'I guess that should have been a dead giveaway.'

As soon as I flopped down on the couch and had patted Marmalade enough to sate her desire for attention, I called Kayleigh.

'I've been waiting for your call all night. Did you kiss?'

I laughed. 'Well, sort of. Which I guess proves my theory about the dreams I analyse in my office coming true.'

'So, tell me all about it.'

'We went to the acting class, and he played Romeo to my Juliet.'

'Ooh, how romantic.'

'It was a lame appropriation of the play and it was the scene where Romeo finds Juliet unconscious. At the end of the scene he kissed me on the mouth.'

'This is gold,' Kayleigh said. 'Tell me more.'

'Well I was playing a virtual corpse, so there wasn't any tongue action or anything.'

'Uh huh.'

'Then after the class Levi asked if I wanted to go for a drink with him at a funky new bar that opened tonight. He's a close friend of the owner Ben. It was the most incredible place I've ever been. We walked straight in, as Levi was on the list, and then we went to the VIP area where we sipped Dom Perignon.'

'Ooh la la.'

'And then Levi made a plan for his lover Ben to come over tonight after the bar closes.'

'Shut up! Are you serious? You mean Levi is

into guys?'

'Yep,' I laughed. 'So, I think we can scrap any dreams about him off the list now.'

'I just can't believe it. The most gorgeous guys are never available.'

'You know what I can't believe is that somehow my life is getting directed by my client's dreams. How am I supposed to live like this? What if someone comes to me with a dream that a crocodile eats them, or that they go skydiving?'

'Or that they eat monkey brains, or that they get eaten alive by a flesh-eating worm.'

'Yep, you get the picture. I think I might have to give up work. But I can't really afford to. What am I going to do?'

'There has to be some way to stop it. I think you should take this week off to rest your ankle and work out a plan of attack. By the way, how is your ankle?'

I looked down to the hot, swollen mess where my ankle should be. 'It's really sore.' I burst into tears, which was out of character for me. I usually only cry at commercials of babies, puppies and kittens.

'Oh, hun. I'm so sorry. It sucks that you're hurt and that things didn't work out with Levi. But think on the bright side. You still have Marmalade to keep you company.'

I looked at the little ginger fluff ball sitting next to me on the lounge licking her genitals. 'I guess,' I replied sniveling.

HOUSE CALL

I flicked through the channels on the television with my remote. None of the content had changed on the stations since the last rotation. So far, the most interesting channel I had found was an Arabic foreign station and I don't even speak Arabic. Every other channel wanted to sell me gimmicky contraptions, was a cheesy game show or repeats of shows from the eighties. The idea of sitting at home watching television or reading a book had seemed heavenly until I was housebound. There was nothing to watch on TV and the only book I'd bought in months had spider guts smeared on the cover and had ended up in the bin, leaving me with nothing to read. The only small amount of satisfaction I had was that I was still in my pyjamas at 5pm, having not bothered getting dressed all day.

The doorbell rang, and I froze. Who would be at my door at this time of day? I looked down at my daggy flannelette pyjamas with teddy bears all over them. There was a small hole in the seam on my leg, which hadn't bothered me enough to sew it up, that was, until this exact moment. My chestnut hair was scooped up in a messy bun and as I hopped to the door, I saw in my reflection in a mirror that on my cheek there were remnants of Nutella, that I may, or may not, have been eating directly from the jar. I licked my finger and wiped away the evidence, even though the jar sat on the coffee table with its lid off and a spoon poking out accusingly.

I cracked the door open a smidge and saw that Sam was standing on the doorstep with a bag of groceries in his hand.

'Uh, hi,' I said, surprised to see my physio on the doorstep.

'Hi. I thought I'd check in on you.'

'I'm good thanks,' I said, still not opening the door to reveal my attire.

'Do you like salmon?' he asked.

'The colour or the fish?' I replied.

'The fish,' he laughed.

'Yes, however, just for the record, apricot and salmon are my most hated colours in the whole spectrum of colours. If you want orange, choose a bright orange, a burnt orange, even tangerine, but apricot and salmon are just insipid.'

Sam laughed. 'Point taken. Well I just bought some fresh salmon and if you don't have plans, I thought I could cook you dinner, since you're convalescing.'

The thought of someone cooking me a meal was far more enticing than trying to maintain my dignity. 'Great, but I'm in my pyjamas and my house is a mess.' I opened the door wide, and he walked in as I hopped back to my place on the lounge.

Marmalade could obviously smell the fish as she leapt up to try to get her claws in Sam's cloth shopping bag. Sam dumped the bag on the kitchen bench and scooped up Marmie to pat her. She snuggled into his chest, purring loudly. She was such a floozy.

Sam placed Marmalade on my lap and knelt in front of my ankle to survey the damage. Since he had treated me the day before, the swelling had subsided a little and the purple bruising had morphed into black.

'It's looking a bit better today,' he said, standing. 'It's not quite as swollen.'

'It still hurts like hell,' I replied.

'I could amputate it for you if you like,' Sam replied with a straight face. 'There's a good second hand black market for donor legs.'

'Funny.' Sam's face was still stoney. 'You are joking, aren't you?' I asked, terrified that I may have just let a serial amputator into my house.

Sam burst into hysterics. 'Oh my god, your face! Don't worry, I'm just kidding.'

Sam walked back into the kitchen to start preparing the meal.

I hopped over to sit on one of my eclectic wooden chairs and propped my leg up on the adjacent chair.

'So, tell me about yourself Samson. For starters is that really your name and did your parents call your sister Delilah?'

'Ha ha. I was born in Fiji and I don't have a sister. However, I do have two half brothers.'

'How old were you when your parents split?' I asked.

'My dad used to work for a diving expedition

company. When I was six, he drowned after the scuba gear malfunctioned when he was diving.'

'Oh, I'm so sorry to hear that. That must have been devastating for you.' I could feel tears welling in my eyes with sorrow for the little six-year-old Sam.

'My mum raised me as a single parent. She always encouraged me to play sports. When I was fourteen, I won a sports scholarship to play rugby at St Swithins College and so I moved to live here in Australia.'

'How sad for your mum to be left all alone. Did she consider moving to be here with you?

'My mum is the only doctor in my village, so she knew she was needed there. She is very selfless and always puts others needs ahead of her own.'

'But how scary for you to move away from home at just fourteen.'

'Yes. It took a while for me to adjust to living here, as life in Australia is very different to Fiji. Everything is rushed and everyone is fueled by desire to own material possessions. Back home things are more chilled, and people just enjoy each other's company. They look out for one another.'

'So why are you still living here then?' I asked.

'After I moved to live in Australia, my mum was very lonely. She ended up meeting my stepdad and they married and now have sons, Josiah and Isaac. Mum has moved on with her life and so I don't really feel like that is home anymore. Plus, I can earn more here and send her money to help with health initiatives for the village.'

'You are such a saint,' I said wistfully.

'Oh no I'm not. As a kid my mum used to think I was a little devil. She put me into rugby to keep me busy and wear me out so I wouldn't trash the house.' He laughed as he reminisced.

'So how long did you play footy?' I asked, reaching down to lift Marmie onto my lap.

'I played professionally for eight years but it is really hard on the body. In 2012, I side stepped to get out of a tackle and I tore my ACL, MCL and meniscus.'

I nodded, although I had no idea what those things were. I didn't want my lack of understanding to get in the way of the story.

'I had to get a knee reconstruction, and I was going to be out of the game for the season. I realised that I couldn't extend my playing career by much longer, so I decided to train to be a physiotherapist.

I graduated and started my business two years ago and it's all going really well.'

'Wow, I really admire you. I sort of just fell into my job. I was halfway through my degree in psychology before I realised that I probably would never become a psychologist. I had no idea how long university would take to become fully qualified.'

While we'd been chatting, Sam had managed to prepare a feast of vegetables. He pulled out the salmon to prepare it. As soon as Marmie got a whiff of it she launched herself at the kitchen bench but fell short. She would never make a good sugar glider.

'Your job sounds interesting. What are some of the strangest dreams you've heard? Keep it PG,' Sam said.

I laughed. 'Surprisingly, not many client's share raunchy dreams with me. It's normally just your run of the mill flying, falling and interactions with family and friends. It's quite interesting that most of the time, the thing you are dreaming about isn't actually anything to do with that exact person or thing. It is all very metaphorical and of course it is open to interpretation. I must admit there are a lot of people who are skeptics.'

'I've seen too many things in my life that can't be explained to dismiss anything.'

'I feel like it really helps people to understand their subconscious thoughts as often it unlocks their true feelings about a situation. I feel like it allows me to use some of what I learned in my psychology degree. I do a slot on the radio once a week and a magazine article once a month. The rest of my time is spent seeing private clients at my office. Most of the time it is a pretty cool job.'

'What don't you like about your job?' Sam asked as he put the salmon on to cook on a hot griddle. I didn't even know that I owned that pan and I certainly didn't know what to use it for. I made a mental note to start using it.

'If I tell you, you'll think I'm crazy.'

'I already think you're crazy, so it won't change anything,' Sam said grinning as his eyebrows wiggled up and down.

'Funny! You have to promise not to judge me if I tell you.'

'I cross my heart I won't judge you, or think you're crazier than I already believe,' Sam replied, using his pointer finger to draw a cross over his heart. I hadn't noticed until that moment just how well his fine woolen jumper hugged his defined pecs. I almost lost my train of thought ogling him. 'So, tell me or I'll just have to think you are a crazy cat lady.'

'I recently noticed that when clients visit me at my office for analysis of their dreams, that parts of their dreams are appearing in my life. For example, the day I found Marmalade, my client had told me a dream about a ginger cat. Another time a client had a dream of falling and then I fell down a flight of stairs. The worst was the other night, after seeing a client that had a dream about spiders; I had a spider crawl across my face while I was asleep. I'm so terrified of what dreams will be projected onto me.'

'Maybe they are just coincidences. I once heard that we all swallow eight spiders in our sleep in our lifetime.'

I shivered involuntarily. 'Okay, now you are really terrifying me. I have arachnophobia so I don't want to ever see a spider again, let alone swallow one.'

'Anyway, from what I know, you are also pretty clumsy, so that would explain the fall.'

I huffed. 'I'm not clumsy, apart from when I'm being chased by a complete stranger wielding a torch in the middle of the night.'

Sam laughed.

'Yesterday I put my theory to the test. I got Kayleigh to come to my office and tell me she'd had a dream of kissing Levi, a model that works in my building.' Sam's smile disappeared, and he leaned back against the kitchen bench and crossed his arms across his chest. 'The next thing I know I'm at an acting class playing Juliet and Levi was Romeo, and he had to kiss me. I'm telling you it's a real thing.'

'So, you're training to become an actress?' Sam asked, turning the salmon.

'No. I just went because Levi wanted company.'

'So, are you and Levi a thing?' Sam asked, concentrating on serving the meals.

'No, he's gay. The thing is, that whatever dream someone gets me to analyse at my office, turns into reality.'

Sam's smile returned as he placed the plates on the dining table. 'So, you're saying you can manipulate what happens to you.'

'It appears so, but it doesn't necessarily happen like it did to the person in the dream.'

'This is fascinating.'

I took a mouthful of the salmon and the flaky texture just melted in my mouth. 'This is delicious. How did you learn to cook like this?'

'I've had to cook for myself since I left boarding school. I never wanted to eat food like that mass-produced slop we got in school ever again. I actually enrolled in a culinary course to learn the basics. I really love food.'

'Oh my god, we are so alike. I love food too,' I said, stating the obvious. 'You don't get these curves without loving food,' I added, hoping I sounded self-deprecating and not just reminding him of my muffin top.

'I like a woman with curves,' Sam said smiling.

I busied myself cutting up my vegetables so I didn't have to look at Sam, as I could feel my face had bloomed a rosy red.

'I was thinking after dinner, maybe, I mean if you're up to it, and I totally understand if you're not,' Sam stammered.

'Come on Sam, spit it out.'

'Well I thought we could go to your office and try out this theory of yours that you are getting other people's dreams becoming your reality. I promise I'll make it a good dream.'

'Just for the record, when you say, "a good dream," I hope that's not code for a wet dream.' As soon as the words were out of my mouth I cringed. I really must learn to think before speaking.

This time it was Sam's turn to blush. He laughed. 'That wasn't what I had in mind. I meant like winning the lottery or something like that.'

'Oh phew. I thought you were trying to be kinky or something.' I laughed as I mentally gave myself an uppercut. I'd only met this guy a few days ago, and I was inferring to him that I thought he was some sleazy creep.

'So, what do you say?' he asked.

'Sure, why not? If nothing else, it will prove to you that I'm not crazy.'

'Or prove to me that you are,' Sam replied with a cheeky grin accompanied by a wink.

Being after hours, Sam was able to park his car on the street directly in front of my office. As we pulled up, I noticed the lights were on in Jason's shop, even though he would have closed for the day hours prior. Work must be really hectic for him to be working back so late. I peered through the shop window and saw the one and only Kween, sitting on the counter next to the register, with a cat that looked like a miniature cheetah in her lap. Jason had told me he was allergic to cats, which was why he had given his ex the ultimatum to choose between him and her cat. He'd also always been adamant that he never wanted pets, but since we had been together, he seemed to have changed his mind about a lot of things. It wasn't that I still pined to be with Jason, but I felt like maybe I had never known the real him. Or maybe Kween Rosy Posy had made such an impact in his life that it had changed him irrevocably.

Sam walked around to open my door and he helped me out of the car, handing me my crutches to hop towards my office. I wasn't sure whether I wanted Jason to look out his shop window and see me. Would he feel a pang of jealousy when he saw me with a handsome stranger, or would he look at me on crutches and laugh at what a klutz I was? Either way, it didn't really matter, as I had moved on with my life and his perception of me was none of my business.

As we reached the stairwell, Sam took my crutches and assisted me up the stairs. I made a note to self: I needed to take Sam everywhere with me as it was much easier than doing the crutches thing on my own.

I opened the door to the office and flicked on the fluorescent overhead lights. Sam walked in behind me. 'That is a stunning dream catcher,' he said, walking over to closely admire my wall decoration.

'Thanks. It is a traditional Native American Indian original.'

'My grandmother used to have a circular wall decoration she made from cowrie shells, cuttlefish bones and feathers. It reminds me of it. I love art that incorporates nature.'

'Me too.' I flopped down onto my seat. 'Okay client, have a seat and tell me your dream.'

I opened my notebook and turned to a new page, as I would if I had a real client.

Sam sat in the chair and leaned back with his hands clasped behind his head. This just accentuated his toned bi-ceps and muscular pecs. I had to make a conscious effort to try to look at his eyes. Not that I was objectifying him…much.

'So, I had a dream that I was in a machine with all these scratchie tickets flying around and I had to snatch one and then scratch it and I won the jackpot amount of money. What does this mean?'

I smiled and put on my most professional voice. 'So, a dream of winning or suddenly coming into money is a sign of confidence. It is your subconscious telling you that it is ready for you to win in real life.'

'Really, or did you make that up?' Sam asked.

'No, that is really what it means.'

'That's cool,' Sam said before leaning forward to whisper, 'How long until this becomes real?'

'It seems to be happening on the same day, but not like people say in their dream. It normally is out of the blue in a completely different scenario.'

'Okay, well I guess my job here is done,' Sam said smiling. 'Thanks for letting me come and check out your office. It's awesome.'

I laughed. 'I'm not sure it's awesome, but it does the job. Just give me a sec to pack up and we can head off.'

After turning off the lights, setting the alarm and locking the door I hobbled to the stairs where Sam again chivalrously helped me down the stairs. As I crossed the foyer, I noticed my letterbox was overflowing. I'd never been too diligent about checking my mail regularly as it was usually mostly junk mail, with a few bills thrown in. As much I would like to ignore the bills, I knew I couldn't, so I quickly emptied the letterbox. I threw the catalogues and other assorted junk mail into a bin, leaving three envelopes personally addressed to me. Two were clearly bills, but the third was a handwritten envelope. I opened the flap of the envelope and retrieved a brightly coloured card with the word 'Thanks' across the cover. Inside was a beautiful handwritten note from my client Judy saying that she had made plans with her friends that included Keith and he seemed to be warming to her friends and had actually enjoyed himself. She was so grateful that I was making a positive difference in her life. My heart swelled with gratitude that she had gone out of her way to let me know that I had been helpful. As I tried to slip the card back into the envelope, it wouldn't fit. When I opened the envelope to see the obstruction, I could see a $5 scratchie had been included with the card. I pulled the scratchie out and held it up to Sam as proof of my life being a reflection of my client's dreams.

'No way! Scratch it and let's see if you have won,' Sam said excitedly. He pulled a loose coin out of his pocket and handed it to me.

I passed my mail to Sam to hold and took his coin. Trying to balance on crutches, I scratched away at the gummy silver coating.

'So, is it a winner?' Sam asked eagerly.

I smiled, waving the scratchie in front of me. 'I

won a free ticket.'

Sam's face dropped. 'Oh. I thought you would win the jackpot, not a free ticket.'

I laughed. 'It's not like what happens to me is a direct replica of the dream, it's just that an element of the dream comes into my life. I'm not too upset. After all, a win is a win. Here, you take this scratchie and redeem the free ticket. You never know, it might win the jackpot. You deserve it. After all, you were the one with the dream.'

Sam smiled. 'I can't take the ticket. That is a gift to you from a happy client.'

'Oh well, don't cry to me if I win a million dollars and it could have been yours,' I replied laughing.

'Come on. I'll take you home. You really need to rest and elevate your foot.'

'Okay Doc,' I replied hobbling towards his car.

Out of the corner of my eye I noticed Jason's shop was still lit up and then I watched as the mini cheetah cat took a dump next to a Play Station display in the front window. A wide grin covered my face. Oh, karma is a bitch. As we drove off, I wondered how long it would take for him to discover his new window decoration.

BED REST

I sat in bed, with my laptop balanced on my lap. I may not be able to get to work with my ankle still swollen the size of a small melon, but I vowed to get on top of this month's magazine article. I pulled up an email containing a few sample dreams that had been sent through by readers. One girl aged sixteen had a dream that she was at school and realised she was in her pyjamas in front of the school assembly. I remember having this type of dream when I was that age. It was common and a sign of feeling vulnerable. I tried to weave some advice into the analysis as this young girl was still on the verge of finding her true identity.

The next dream was from a middle-aged woman. I wasn't sure why she was reading and writing in to a magazine called *Teen Girl*, except that she had once been a teen girl. She wrote that she had a recurring dream that she was taking an exam in school, even though she hadn't been in school for over three decades. She said she woke up feeling stressed and sweating profusely. My research had shown that a dream of sitting for tests was usually had by someone that was a high achiever. They wanted to excel at everything and so their subconscious was constantly putting pressure on them to be a perfectionist.

The final email was from a girl who said she dreamed of dying and had been unable to shake the feeling of overwhelming unease. Reading this dream took my breath away. My heart began racing, and I had a sinking feeling in my stomach. Thank God this dream was a written one and not a client sitting at my work. What was I going to do if someone came to me with this in person and it transferred to me? How was I going to be able to do my job if I was constantly running the risk of nightmares becoming my reality? I took a deep breath. For the moment I just needed to do my job and finish my assessment. The good thing for this girl was that a dream of dying rarely had anything to do with death. It was usually a sign that you craved a change in lifestyle, such as a new project, new relationship or a change of location. I finished my article and emailed it to the magazine.

As soon as I heard the whooshing noise that signaled the email had been sent, my thoughts immediately resumed ruminating over how I could continue my job. Marmalade jumped up on my bed, surprising me, not only with the fact that she could now reach the bed, but she also had a strand of wool in her mouth. I looked at the bright pink wool. I hadn't given her any wool to play with. The colour of the wool was vaguely familiar. I leaned to look out my bedroom doorway into the lounge room and saw the remnants of a pink woolen sweater strewn around the room. Marmie had obviously managed to pull on a loose thread, which had then unraveled one side of my jumper. The pile of wool resembled neon pink spaghetti thrown around the room like a Pro Hart carpet cleaning commercial from my youth. I picked up the single strand of wool that Marmie had brought to me and dangled it in front of her. She pounced like a lion targeting its prey. How easily she was distracted, I thought, then realised her distraction had once again distracted me. A ruined jumper paled into insignificance when my life could be in mortal danger if I continued my career. But not having a job and money to pay for food and shelter would also impact being able to live.

My phone beeped, momentarily drawing my attention away from my impending doom. I retrieved it to find a text message from Sam.

How is your ankle today?

> *It's getting better. Thanks again for dinner last night.*

My pleasure. I still can't believe your clients' dreams become your reality. It was crazy after I told you about winning a lottery that within minutes you won on a scratchie.

> *I'm scared to go back to work. What happens if someone has a really bad dream, and that becomes my new reality? I just don't think I can work again.*

You can't let fear rule your life. Maybe you need to warn clients that they can't tell you dreams that have themes of death or permanent injury.

> *Don't you think that will make me look like an imbecile?*

You have to do whatever will protect you until you work out why this is happening. In the meantime, you need to try to exploit this as best you can.

Haha. Like what?

Well you could have a friend come and tell you they dreamed of going on a date with a hunky Fijian physiotherapist and then I would be compelled to take you out.

Are you asking me on a date or is that just an example?

If you would like to go on a date, I'm happy to oblige. If not, it can just be an example.

I'm not opposed to going on a date with you. What do you have in mind?

I was going to suggest going bungee jumping, but given your ankle is still sore, would you like to go see a movie tomorrow night?

That would be great.

I'll leave the movie and time up to you. I should be finished with my clients by 5.30pm, so any time after that. Just let me know what suits.

Okay

For at least two minutes I added a kiss to the end of the message, then deleted it in case it seemed too desperate, but then again, I wanted him to know I was interested in him, but not too interested. It was getting to the point of my worrying that he would think that I wasn't going to respond, so I took a deep breath and throwing caution to the wind I added 'x' to the end of my message and hit send.

A ridiculous grin had spread across my face. I hadn't found a solution to my problem with work, but suddenly my mind was no longer worried about my job killing me. My first priority was to research movies and session times. I enjoyed watching lighthearted rom-coms but worried that it would be too girly for a big burly guy like Sam. There was some comic book hero installment, which to be honest, I would rather stick hot pokers in my eyes than watch. I just didn't get peoples' fascination with seeing movies of cartoons come to life. If that film was Sam's movie of choice, then I would have to tell him honestly that he had failed to meet my minimum standard of compatibility and that we could no longer be friends. I settled on a psychological thriller that would hopefully entertain us both.

Is the 8pm session tomorrow night of Girl in the Mirror okay?

Great. It's a date x

My breath caught. Sam had added a kiss to the end of his message, without any delay. Okay, so I might die when I returned to work next week, but at least I would die happy.

RAIN CHECK

As rain drizzled down the windowpane, I had focused my efforts on pampering. I had spent the better part of two hours lazing in the bath. My ankle had turned a lovely rainbow of yellow and green, a sign that it was healing, and its swelling had reduced, leaving it almost the same size as my other cankle.

I dangled my finger over the edge of the bath long enough to distract Marmie from attacking the bathmat. She leapt at my finger, missing it narrowly.

'Oh, you're a cheeky girl,' I said, my voice cracking.

Marmalade had lost interest in the bathroom and wandered off towards the lounge room. I hoped that maybe this was a sign she was toilet trained and desperately hoped that I wouldn't find a little surprise puddle when I got out of the bathtub.

With music playing softly in the background and scented candles on the vanity, I lathered my hair and washed it to make it look glossy for my imminent date with Sam. I used a loofah, that had sat in the back of my cupboard for years gathering dust, to scrub away decades of dead cells from my skin. It left my skin red raw, but smoother than I recalled it ever feeling. With six hours until our date, I was banking on my skin returning to a normal shade. Either that, or dressing up like a lobster to take advantage of my new skin tone.

With the bath water cooling and only lukewarm water coming out of the hot tap, I decided to remove my wrinkly body from the water and move onto phase two of drying and styling my hair.

The phone rang and seeing that it was Sam, I lurched, rather painfully, towards it.

'Hi Sam,' I said, trying to disguise the sound of the pain I felt from overworking my ankle.

'Hey Maggie. How are you?' Sam's voice sounded uncharacteristically quiet.

'I'm good. I'm really looking forward to our date tonight.'

There was a pause. 'Um, just about that. I'm sorry but I have to cancel. I'm on the way to the airport. My mum called earlier to let me know my grandma passed away last night in her sleep. I have to go to Fiji for the funeral.'

'I'm so sorry to hear that. How is your mum coping?'

'She is okay. It is my grandma on my dad's side.'

'Were you close?'

'She was the most incredible woman, but you know with me living here since I was fourteen, I haven't been the best grandson. I haven't seen her for over two years.' His voice began to crack with emotion.

'I'm sure she would have been so proud of you.'

'Thank you.'

'There is nothing like weddings and funerals to bring family back together. Make the most of your time seeing your relatives.'

'I will. I'll let you know when I'm back so we can go see that movie another night.'

'Okay. Safe travels.'

'Bye.'

My skin had blossomed into a sea of goose bumps. I threw aside the clothes I had chosen to wear on our date and instead put on my tracksuit. I looked at my reflection in the mirror and saw a sad, bloated version of myself. Granted, my wet hair looked slick after its treatment, but even so, there was more to attraction than just glossy hair. Maybe Sam had cold feet and was using a funeral as a ruse to get out of dating me. As much as he said he liked women with curves, I knew it was time to start taking care of myself. I couldn't start running or doing any cardio workouts with my ankle still recovering, but I really wanted to change my ways. The meal Sam had made the other night had shown me that you could eat tasty meals that were healthy too. I lay on the floor, determined to start exercising in some way. As I started to do some sit-ups, Marmie pounced on me, not wanting to miss out on the commotion. I snuggled with Marmie, laughing at her wriggling in my lap, my exercise plans for the day put on the back burner.

I instead headed into the kitchen, and while the motivation was strong, I began to toss out all my unhealthy food. I started with the ice-cream in my freezer. Ice-cream was overrated – seconds on the lips, lifetime on the hips. I then emptied my cupboards of all my packets of Tim Tams. I threw away the chocolate original packet, the double chocolate packet, the dark chocolate packet, the mint infused packet and the caramel packet. Who knew I'd been guilty of hoarding so many biscuits? I threw away the half-eaten block of chocolate in the fridge and finally reached for the jar of Nutella. My days of feeding myself the hazelnut chocolatey goodness were gone. I closed the bin lid and felt a mixture of satisfaction that I had such will power and a sudden surge of craving for chocolate. I turned to walk away and then totally undermining my will power, I opened the bin and reached for the jar of Nutella. I unscrewed the lid and dipped my finger into the smooth spread, before my self-control could register what I was doing. Once my finger was fully laden with the sugary food of the gods, I placed it in my mouth and sucked the delicious hazelnut chocolate spread off, savouring its velvety sweet texture for one last time.

I held the jar of Nutella up in the air. 'Farewell dear Nutella, I will never forget our time together. You have been my constant companion, but it is time to end this needy relationship. It's not you, it's me. It's time I move forward with my life.'

I screwed the lid back on the jar and threw it into the bin. I then removed the bag from the bin and tied a knot in the top to stop myself if I had another lapse in conscience. Then to be sure, I did a second knot, because I knew I could be a crafty bugger if my sugar addiction got the better of me. I then hobbled to the front door and down to the wheely bin and threw away the bag containing my bad habits. This was the only way to guarantee my resolve as there was no way I would scrounge around in a wheely bin for a chocolate fix.

Over the next few days my ankle was able to weight bare and I managed to limp around without crutches, which came as a relief in terms of time management but more so, my ribs were bruised where the crutches had been pushing in as I walked. It's not until your health takes a dive that you actually stop taking good health for granted. I made a mental note to wake up every morning and feel gratitude for all the parts of my body that were functioning as they should. I religiously did the exercises Sam had given me to help strengthen my ankle, and they seemed to make a difference.

When bin collection night rolled around again, I went out under the cover of darkness once more, deciding to look further afield in search of the cat dumper. I snuck from the bin to bin around the whole block. Green, orange and white bin liners galore, but no-one seemed to use purple bin liners. I had slightly changed my opinion on whether those lavender scented bags were a bad thing. After sniffing the stench from all those bins, some lavender filling my nostrils would have been a welcome reprieve.

I returned home feeling deflated. I hadn't found any evidence to link anyone to Marmalade's dumping, and I hadn't heard from Sam, which magnified my insecurity of him maybe getting cold feet. I did happen to walk past his house, relieved to see no lights on and his bin was still sitting on his side path. I looked inside the bin to see there was one lone garbage bag. I wheeled his bin to the curb before I continued home.

As I lay in bed, contemplating my return to work the following morning, a kaleidoscope of butterflies was fluttering in my belly. I had to work out why my clients' dreams were infiltrating my life and how to stop it. In the interim, I had decided to take Sam's advice and ask clients to not share with me dreams of death and destruction. I planned on telling them it triggered me and hoped they would respect my request. That would just leave me open to every other thing on the planet. The thought made me feel queasy and weak at the knees.

Marmie had given up the pretense of sleeping in the cat bed. Now that she could easily jump on my bed, she had taken over the mattress. I lay on my side with Marmie curled in the crook of my knees. Her warmth was a comfort at a time when I was feeling vulnerable.

Needing a distraction, I googled Samson Telavatu. I'm normally much better on my stalking game than I had been the last few weeks. I was shocked that I hadn't tried to find out more about Sam before this. Sam had obviously been very humble when talking with me about his career. Not only did he have the record as the highest try scorer in rugby union in the schoolboys' competition, but he had played for the NSW Waratahs in the Australian national competition. As if that wasn't a high enough achievement, he had freaking played test matches for Fiji, captaining the team before his retirement. Oh my god - he even had his own Wikipedia page. I switched to images, and I felt like I'd been punched in the gut. There were photos of him with his local team and his national team, photos of him flanked by middle-aged female fans, but the ones that drew my interest were the ones of him with supermodels who were six foot tall and rake thin, draping themselves over him. He looked like the cat that ate the cream with his Cheshire cat grin. There were photos of him at black tie events, each one accompanied by a glamorous girl or at the very least, a mildly famous pop star. There were literally hundreds of photos of him. I'd been hanging out with a famous sports star and I hadn't even realised. No wonder he had gone M.I.A. He was probably in bed with some Victoria's Secret model and had forgotten all about me. I shut my laptop and turned out the light. I had to return to work tomorrow and knowing that I would have to deal with my client's dream, I had to feel well rested.

DAYDREAM

I had been giving myself a pep talk all morning. I knew I could handle whatever my day held. As I entered my office, I was suddenly overtaken with a swell of pride. To think I had established this business by myself and earned enough to pay the bills gave me great satisfaction. I suddenly burst into singing 'Independent Women' by Destiny's Child. I may not have a husband and children, or even a boyfriend for that matter, but I didn't need to rely on anyone. I was successful in my own right. Go girl power!

I sat at my desk and booted up my computer. I quickly replied to a few booking requests before my first client for the day entered. It was Lynette, a bubbly outgoing petite woman in her forties, who had been to see me a few times over the past year.

'Hi, Lynette. How are you?'

'I'm well. How have you been?'

'I've been on crutches over the past few weeks. I sprained my ankle quite badly, but it's on the mend now.'

'Sounds serious. I hope you are okay.'

'I'm fine. I'm just a bit clumsy it seems.' I smiled and took a deep breath. 'Lynette, before we start our session, can I please request that you don't share with me any dreams about death or destruction. As I empathise with people's dreams, I can find those types of dreams quite triggering and I have to look after myself. I'm sure you understand.'

'Oh, of course. I totally get it.'

'Great, so why don't you tell me the dream you would like me to analyse today.'

'Well I had a dream the other night that I was in this beautiful orchard in Valencia in Spain. I went there in my twenties and did a season of fruit picking. The aroma of citrus always takes me back there. Anyway, in my dream the orchard was full of small bees. I wasn't scared of the bees, but instead was in awe of them. It left me feeling quite enlightened. What do you think this means?'

I silently assessed in my mind whether I had any allergy to bees. While I wasn't happy with the thought that a bee might suddenly attack me, it was better than being hit by a car.

'Well Lynette, the reason you felt enlightened is that a dream of bees is a sign of happiness and good fortune, particularly on the work front. Do you know the saying "busy bees"?' Lynette nodded. 'Bees symbolize diligence and hard work and you can soon hope to benefit from the result of your efforts. Are you up for a promotion or an extension of your duties at work?'

Lynette's face lit up. 'Now that you mention it, there is talk of a restructure at my work and I do get good feedback from my boss. I have been hoping that I might be considered for a promotion.'

'It is amazing what your subconscious wants to tell you when you are asleep. All I can say is keep up your hard work and you will reap the rewards.'

'I just love coming to see you. You give me so much clarity. I've been recommending you to all my friends.'

'Thanks. That's so kind.'

We discussed Lynette's work and her job prospects for a while. Glancing at the clock, I realized the session needed to be wrapped up. 'Good luck with the promotion. Do you want to book in for another session in a few months?'

'That would be great. Maybe a Monday in three months time.'

I booked in her next session and after she left I returned to my desk. As soon as I sat down, I could hear a buzzing noise coming from the window. With dread I turned towards the source of the noise. To my relief it was just a blow fly buzzing around the windowsill. I exhaled, glad to have avoided an encounter with a bee for the meantime.

No sooner had I finished with Lynette's notes than my next client arrived. Veronica entered the room and sat down nervously. She was an athletic powerhouse of a woman who would look more at home on a running track than sitting perched on my vinyl chair. Her knees jiggled as she placed her hands on her thighs, looking like she was trying to keep her legs still.

'I'm sorry, I've never done this before. I'm not sure if you're going to tell me something bad about my dreams that will change my life.'

I laughed. She was worried I was going to tell her something bad – I was far more concerned that she was going to tell me a bad dream that would ruin my life.

'I'm not a psychic about to make predictions. All I do is listen to your dream and then interpret what your own subconscious is trying to tell you. I do ask that you don't share any dreams about death or permanent disablement.'

Veronica struggled to sit still.

'Before we talk about your dreams, would you like to tell me a bit about yourself? It might make it easier for me to hone in on the correct interpretation for your dream.'

Veronica relaxed slightly. 'Okay. I'm thirty-seven and I work as a personal trainer. I'm a single mother of two boys who keep me busy. On alternate weekends when the boys stay with their dad I usually train or race in triathlons.'

'Wow, that's impressive. I thought you looked fit. I've been recovering from a sprained ankle, but I'm keen to start getting fit. Do you have any advice?'

Veronica's eyes roamed my body, as if seeing me for the first time. 'I would start with running. There's nothing like a good cardio workout to shed kilos.'

I nodded; embarrassed that she had automatically assumed that by saying I wanted to get fit that what

I actually meant was that I wanted to lose weight. 'That's good to know,' I replied. 'Okay, how about you tell me about your dream?'

'I feel like my dream is self explanatory, but my PT client Daisy saw you a few weeks ago and said that you offered her a new outlook on life after you analysed her dream. Anyway, my dream is that I'm running, but it's not like I'm just going out for a casual jog, it's like I'm running like I'm being chased, although I don't know what I'm running from.'

I nodded. Okay, I can do running and in fact this dream will serve as good motivation to start my exercise routine.

'Well, running is a very interesting dream as it can have several meanings. You can be running away from something or running towards a goal. I feel that since you say you feel like you're being chased that you are running from something. How long have you and your ex-husband been separated?'

'It's almost six months. I caught the scumbag cheating on me with a sales rep from his work.'

'I get the sense that you want to be free from the marriage and are trying to distance yourself. Have you finalized your financial settlement yet?'

'No. We are meeting with a mediator in two weeks. Craig is being really unreasonable with the division of assets. We wouldn't even be in this mess if he had been faithful.'

'So, it seems to me that you want to distance yourself from your marriage and are chasing the goal of full independence. It is also an apt symbol as you gain your pleasure from running. I'll be interested to see if you continue having running dreams after settlement and whether they morph into leaving you with a sense of freedom, rather than feeling like you are being chased.'

Tears pooled in Veronica's eyes. 'I truly thought you would say I was wasting your time and that because I like running, I dream of running. The truth is I do feel anxious all the time, like this divorce is always hanging over my head. I do want to be free of it and be able to get closure so I can move on with my life.' I discreetly pushed a box of tissues in Veronica's direction. There weren't really any words that would help change her situation.

'How is your sleep going? Are you suffering any insomnia?' This really had nothing to do with dream analysis, but I could see Veronica needed someone to talk to.

'I'm so exhausted at the end of the day, as I try to work out as hard as possible to help me sleep. I fall straight asleep, but then around 1am, I'm wide-awake with thoughts, and I mean angry thoughts, running through my head. The longer I lie there, the angrier I get. I just don't understand why he would cheat. Why throw away our whole family to sleep with a gold-digging whore?'

'Were you having problems prior to finding out about the affair?' I knew I was in the psychology arena, but it wasn't like I was charging her as a psychologist so surely it was okay to help her.

'I was totally blindsided. I mean, we went through good times and bad times, but I always thought we were a team. I knew he was working late more often, but he always reassured me it was so he could get a promotion to help pay down the mortgage quicker. I never realised those late nights were booty calls to his colleague.'

'You were understandably angry and shocked by the break down of your marriage. How do you feel about it now?'

'I'm still really sad that Craig could have done this, but to be honest, I'm past pining the marriage. I want to be able to move on. I'm just doing my best to try to stay civil with him for the sake of the kids. It's been a hard adjustment period for them too. Like it or not, Craig and I will have to be linked together through our kids for the rest of our lives.

At least the one thing we can agree on is that we want our split to have as little impact on the kids as possible. Outwardly they seem to be coping okay, but I do worry about the long-term effects. Actually, I should bring my son Archie in to see you. He wakes up every morning eager to share his wild dreams with anyone who will listen. Maybe his dreams might give me an insight to how he is really coping.'

'As I've said, dreams are our subconscious releasing our true anxieties and feelings about situations. I'm happy to have a session with him if he is keen.'

'Thank you so much for your time today. I feel like I've been in therapy and had a weight lifted off my shoulders.'

Once Veronica left, I heaved a sigh of relief. I could cope with today's dreams, even though the thought of being stung by a bee was a bit nerve racking. I typed up notes from my client sessions and got prepared for the phone conference with the radio station the following morning.

When I got home, I intended on going for a run, and when I say run, I mean a slow jog/fast walk. Today was as good a day as any to start getting fit.

Given Veronica's dream of running, I hoped that by purposely running, it would stop any situation where I might be chased. If dreams were open to interpretation, then surely their effect on me should be too.

As I parked my car in front of my home, I noticed my neighbour's curtains flick back. Nosy Norman, my neighbour in the adjacent villa, was a grumpy old man with too much time on his hands. I tried to jog towards my front door, just as he opened his door.

'Hello Maggie. I'm just getting my mail,' Nosy Norman said as justification for ambushing me.

'Hi, Norman. How are you?'

'Well my knee has been playing up. Thankfully we are almost into spring. The warmer weather will help.'

'Oh well. Look after yourself,' I replied, turning to put my key in the lock of my door.

'While I've got you - do you think you could do something about your lawn? It's overgrown with weeds.'

I restrained my eyes from rolling. My lawn was the size of a handkerchief and if I had a lawn mower, it would take a whole two minutes to mow, but as I didn't have a lawnmower, I would have to get out and hand cut the grass. I cast my eyes over the patch of turf, or more precisely weeds, and was struck by the fact that I hadn't noticed how pretty it looked with the yellow blooms of dandelions dancing in the light wind. It was like a mini meadow of wildflowers. Wasn't it morally wrong to remove weeds, as they were integral to the survival of bees?

Nosy Norman was waiting on my reply.

'Okay Norman, I'll do that. You take care of yourself.' I quickly darted inside the house and shut the door firmly behind me, blocking out Nosy Norman and his annoying complaint about my lawn.

The more I thought about his complaint, the angrier I got. A plan formulated in my mind. I had never been a greenie, but it was never too late to start looking out for bees. I turned on my computer and a laminator that I had stored in the top of my wardrobe. I then found tape and bamboo skewers. Within half an hour I was ready to execute my plan.

I opened the door and walked to my mini meadow. Bees were flitting from one dandelion flower to the next. It would be cruel to ruin their food supply chain and to be honest, being a lover of honey, what goes around comes around. I would benefit from the local bees being able to tend their hives.

I taped miniature signs that I had laminated onto the skewers and erected them around the yard. 'Buzz Off,' 'Keep off the grass, bees at work,' 'To bee or not to bee, that is the question,' 'Make honey not war' and 'Don't disturb the busy bees.' Problem solved – no need to mow, and I was saving the environment at the same time. Without wanting to brag, I was a total genius. As I hurried back towards my front door, I noticed the curtain in the front window next door twitch again. I quickly ducked back inside my house and then ran to my bedroom window to watch Nosy Norman come out to inspect what I had done. He bent down and squinted at the miniature signs. His face screwed up more with each mini placard he read. He shook his head and even though I was inside, I could hear him exhale a loud huff. I quietly giggled and went to cuddle Marmie who was in the process of clawing at the side of my lounge in an attempt to make it look even shabbier than ever before.

Knowing that Norman usually ate dinner around 5.30pm, I waited until he would be preoccupied with that to leave to go on my run. It was the first time I could remember actually being active in active wear. I jogged down the street and noticed Sam's lights were on. My heart gave a little flutter. I argued with myself over whether I should go knock on his door to say hi, but decided I didn't want to seem like a stage five clinger. If Sam were keen, he would have contacted me. I ran faster, just in case he happened to look out the window and admired my amazing running style. He might even question why I hadn't become an Olympic sprinter. By the time I got around the corner, about one hundred metres from his house, I could barely breathe. A painful stitch ran up the left side of my torso. I stopped and hunched over, trying to catch my breath. I walked the rest of the way around the block and exactly eight minutes after leaving my home I had returned, my exercise for the day complete.

I retrieved my phone from the weird pocket at the back of my tights. I had run/walked eight hundred metres, burned thirty-two calories and had no missed calls from Sam. Maybe he was getting over jetlag and would call in the morning, or maybe he was entertaining some super model, or maybe he just wasn't that into me. I flopped down on the lounge, exhausted from my run. My ankle ached a bit, but no more than all the other muscles on my body that were also not used to this thing called exercise.

Instead of having a pity party over being ignored by the one hot guy that had ever shown me the slightest bit of interest in my whole life, I decided instead to reflect on the good things that had happened with my day. I felt like I had helped my clients, I had been motivated to start exercising, I had a cute ginger fluff ball that got enjoyment from pouncing on my feet and I had made a stand on behalf of the bees. Come to think of it, my noble actions to help save the bees (and save me mowing) must have been my bee interaction from the dream. I had dodged being stung by a bee. All in all, there was nothing to bee sad about. I half grinned/half groaned at my own pun.

DREAM HOLIDAY

I phoned the radio station from home. Having heard there was a traffic jam on the main road between my home and my office, I didn't want to risk missing the time slot for my dream session.

I was on hold, doodling mandalas on a scrap of paper, as I listened to Davey and Charlie chatting on the radio.

'We have Maggie McIntyre, the dream guru, coming up soon. In the meantime, call us with the locations of your dream holiday,' Davey said in his slick DJ voice.

Charlie then interjected, 'If I could go anywhere, I would go stay in one of those over water bungalows in the Maldives. Imagine waking up surrounded by nothing but crystal clear, aqua water.'

'That would be my idea of hell,' Davey replied. 'I hate the heat. Anytime I end up somewhere tropical, my body gets covered in this mangy heat rash. I just end up spending my time in the bar. My idea of a dream holiday is skiing in Japan, carving up powder, under blue bird skies.'

Suddenly the phone line stopped playing the on-hold radio. 'Hey Maggie, we know you will be along soon to analyse our audience's dreams, but can you tell us what your dream holiday location would be?' Charlie asked.

Put on the spot, I just said the first thing to come to mind. 'Uh, that's a tough one. Maybe an island in Fiji. I could do with sipping cocktails by a pool while reading a good book.'

Charlie piped up, 'There you go Davey. Tropical holidays are far more appealing than winter holidays. Let's go to our callers to see what locations they say.'

They opened up the phone lines and discussed all the wonderful locations people desired to travel. Back on hold, I worried that if Sam had been listening, he might have misinterpreted my answer as a way to tell him I wanted him to take me home to visit his family. Why couldn't I just have said Tahiti?

The phone line went live again. 'So, we are taking ten lucky listeners on an all expenses paid holiday. The first ten callers who said tropical locations are getting four days staying on the newly refurbished Daydream Island in the Whitsundays, this weekend.'

'You know what would be even better,' Charlie said, 'if Maggie could come along and do some dream sessions. What do you say Maggie?'

I was shocked. Who in their right mind would give up the opportunity for an all expenses paid trip to a tropical island? 'I would love to.'

'Great. You can take my place Maggie, because I can't think of anything worse. No offence to Daydream Island, I'm sure it's amazing, but it's just not my thing,' Davey said.

'Perfect. It's a girl's trip then,' Charlie said.

'Sounds good. It's a dream come true,' I replied, happy with my pun.

'So Davey, you just keep the home fires burning and we will have a cocktail in your honour.'

'Look at you gloating. Don't worry, next year the station will have to give away a trip to Japan and then you'll be left here all on your lonesome.'

'Look at the time, we are running really late this morning. I guess we had better get on with

"Dreamtime" with Maggie McIntyre.' The musical intro, a mash up of songs with lyrics using the word dream played.

I felt relaxed, knowing that when I analysed dreams remotely, they didn't affect me.

'So, we have Roy on the line. Roy tell us your dream,' Davey said.

'I had this really weird dream last night that I was trapped in the corner of a dark room while a rat tried to gnaw at me.'

'Mate, that's not a dream. That is an out-and-out nightmare. What do you have to say about this one Maggie?' Davey asked.

'Okay Roy, the rat symbolizes a threat, so feeling trapped by a rat may mean that there is someone you don't trust that is making you feel threatened and you feel trapped in that situation. Does this make sense to you?'

'Yep,' Roy replied.

'Want to tell us a bit about it?' Davey enquired.

'Not really,' Roy laughed nervously.

'We should guess who is threatening Roy,' Charlie said lightly.

'My money is on a woman,' Davey replied.

'Maybe Roy is a spy or a drug mule,' Charlie said laughing.

Roy didn't respond. The last thing I wanted was for him to feel publicly humiliated. I interjected, 'We're running late. I think we should move on to the next caller.'

'Okay, we have Michelle on the line,' Charlie said.

'Hi, Michelle. What's your dream?'

'I keep having a dream that I'm in an airplane that is flying very low to the ground. It doesn't crash or anything. I'm hoping it means I'm going on a trip. In fact, are there any more spots to go to Daydream Island?'

'Ha ha, I'm afraid not,' Charlie replied.

'Michelle, a dream of flying doesn't have anything to do with travel,' I replied.

'Damn,' Michelle said laughing.

'It actually symbolizes being very grounded. It means that even though you set goals for yourself, you are realistic.'

'Except about getting the free holiday,' Davey

interjected. Everyone laughed.

'You are very down to earth and reliable. If you do want to go on a holiday, you are the sort of person to plan it, save and budget for it, then book it, knowing the entire itinerary before you go.'

Michelle laughed, 'Yep, that sounds like me.'

'What do you do for a job?' I asked.

'I'm an executive assistant,' Michelle replied.

'So, organization and being realistic are really important in that job. Your dreams are just reaffirming that you are in the right career.'

'Thanks for that. I'm a bit disappointed it doesn't mean I'm going on a holiday, but you are right, if I were to go on holiday, I would want to plan every second before I book.'

'We have time for one more caller. Rosemary, tell us your dream,' Davey said.

'Hello. I had a dream my boyfriend died,' Rosemary replied in a husky voice, like she had smoked a packet of cigarettes a day since birth.

'Did you kill him, or was it natural causes?' Davey asked.

'I didn't kill him,' she replied humourlessly.

My first thought was that I was grateful a dream about death happened over the phone and not in person. I shivered involuntarily. The name Rosemary also made me feel uneasy, as there was a chance I was talking with Jason's new/old girlfriend. Then again, it could be any other woman called Rosemary. I had to be professional, so I took a deep breath to calm myself.

'Rosemary, to dream of a death doesn't mean there is an impending death. It signifies a change to something, possibly an end to a relationship or job. It might be a restructure at work or moving out of your current role. What do you do for work?'

'I don't work,' she replied curtly.

'Well, maybe it's an end to the period of not working. Maybe there is a job on the horizon for you,' I said with an upbeat voice.

'No,' Rosemary replied.

'Maybe it is the end of being in the same location and you will be making a change to where you live?'

'I don't think so.'

I wondered why she called in when she seemed so unhelpful in trying to work out the link between the dream and her life. Usually people wanted to give you way too much information.

'Okay, well I will leave the interpretation up to you to work out. Thanks for calling in.'

'Yeah. I'm not sure you know anything about dreams, really. I think you're just there for a hoax.'

My eyes opened wide, shocked at the outburst.

'Okay. Well you don't have to take any notice of what I've said. That is completely up to you. Most people agree with my analysis, but if you don't, that is fine.' I could feel my body shaking with rage and hoped that my voice wasn't quivering. Why would she attack me for no apparent reason?

Davey interjected, 'Well you have a good day Rosemary and maybe next time you call, make sure you haven't got out of the wrong side of the bed. Well folks, that's all we have time for today. Tune in again tomorrow morning for more of the breakfast show with Charlie and Davey.'

As the music for the end of the show played Davey spoke to me. 'That last chick was hard work. I reckon she probably did just stab some guy in the back.'

'It was a bit of an outburst wasn't it? I understand that sometimes it takes a while for the interpretation to make sense to people, but that wasn't cool calling me a hoaxer.'

Beth, the producer came on the line. 'Sorry to toss you in at the deep end live on air Maggie. Are you okay to do the trip this weekend?'

'I'm super keen,' I replied, happy to divert my attention away from the bitterness of the last caller and focus on my free holiday.

'Okay, I'll email all the details to you. Do you think you could do a half-hour session with each of the winners?'

'That's fine. I'll have to pull out my summer clothes. I'm really excited.'

'That's good. I was worried that we might have stepped over the line by putting you on the spot.'

'Not at all. I'm thrilled to go.'

Kayleigh agreed to take Marmalade for the weekend which left me with just trying to find clothes suitable for strutting around a tropical island and to put aside time to do some personal grooming. I welcomed the distraction to stop me thinking about Sam and the reasons he hadn't contacted me since his return.

I decided to go for another run as my muscles had just stopped aching from my previous run/walk. I had a different plan this time, to run slower but further. I pulled on my active wear again and sprinted past Nosy Norman's place. As soon as I was twenty metres from his boundary, I relaxed into a casual jog. I didn't turn my head to look at Sam's house as I passed, but in my periphery, I could see his blinds were up, which was a sign he was definitely back from Fiji. I managed to jog halfway around the block before needing to slow to a fast walk. When I returned home, I was pleased when the health app on my phone showed I had burned thirty-five calories – three more calories than my last run. I was making progress. At this rate, I would be able to run a marathon by the time I turned sixty.

I turned on the shower and looked at my reflection in the bathroom mirror. Cutting the junk food out of my diet over the past week or so seemed to be making a difference. The size of my muffin top looked like it might have shrunk a little, or maybe it was just that active wear was designed to sculpt your body in all the right places. I went to remove my sports bra, an almost impossible task where I managed to get the back of it stuck between my shoulder blades, with my arms trapped by the straps in a position over my head. I wriggled the bra

from side to side, almost amputating one of my
breasts in the process. Eventually I managed to get
out of the contortionist position and freed myself
from the constraints of the bra. I'm sure I worked
up more of a sweat doing this than the actual
exercise that had come before. Marmie, who had
watched the whole debacle, stared at me with a look
of disdain and then twisted herself up into an
equally ridiculous position and began to lick herself.

Thursday night I decided was the time for a
beauty overhaul in readiness for my tropical
getaway. My legs had a reptilian look about them
after being mostly ignored for the winter months. I
shaved and moisturized them, making the skin on
my legs a smooth, shiny gloss white. I then applied
self-tanner, because I certainly didn't want to blind
the guests with glare off my legs. Four hours later
my skin was a bronzed gold, except for the wrinkly
skin on my elbows, knees and knuckles, which had
turned a deep ochre tone. I tried in vain to scrub the
tanning lotion off my knuckles but noticed that it
wasn't budging from the fine lines of my fingers
and toes; however, the surrounding tan was
beginning to lighten. What was better: to have pale
patches of skin but no staining on my knuckles, or
have golden tanned skin and oompa loompa
knuckles? I decided that I was being paranoid, and I

was best to just leave the tan as it was, because realistically who was going to be looking at my hands?

When I arrived at the airport the following morning, the radio producer Beth, Charlie and ten excited couples greeted me. Charlie was also sporting a fake tan. I instantly looked at her hands – damn it, she must have got a professional tan. I watched her smirk as she looked at my hands; she'd noticed my rookie error. I crossed my arms and shoved my hands in under my armpits to hide them from view.

'Welcome to your dream holiday everyone,' Charlie said in her professional announcer voice into a wireless microphone. It never ceased to amuse me how her voice changed between her work voice and her casual normal voice. She had somehow managed to create a deep husky voice that had rounded vowels and oozed calmness and confidence. Off air, Charlie's voice was loud and a bit squeaky. There was going to be a live cross to the radio station until we boarded the plane and then the radio crew would take a few sound bites of people enjoying their holiday over the next few days. All I had to do was give each guest a half-hour session and the rest of the time was mine to do whatever I pleased.

After checking in to my luxurious room, I changed into a summery dress. The temperature was in the high twenties, but having just come out of winter, it felt like I was in a heat wave. I walked over to the pool where I could see Charlie lying in the shallows of the lagoon pool, in a skimpy white bikini. If I did that, people might mistake me for a beached whale and throw me into the ocean. I sat by the edge of the pool and put my feet in the water to help cool my core temperature. The water was temperate and smelled strongly of chlorine, which is a great thing to dilute kids' pee. What kid in the history of the world could be bothered getting out of the pool to go to the toilet when they could just pee where they were? My best friend in primary school used to have a swimming pool at her home. Her dad always told me he used a chemical that turned blue if someone peed in the water. It wasn't until I was in my late teens that I found out that it was a ruse. I could still remember a sign that was by the pool, where most responsible pool owners would have a safety sign showing CPR. It read, 'Welcome to our ool. Notice there is no p in it – let's keep it that way.' His joke had trained me well but had also made me paranoid about swimming in pools where kids were playing.

I relaxed, soaking in the warmth of the sun. I wasn't entirely sure how I had managed to fall into a position of being given a free tropical holiday, but I certainly wasn't complaining.

'So, Maggie, have you got a partner?' Charlie asked, looking like a beautiful mermaid as she glided over to me.

'No, I'm single,' I replied self-consciously.

'You're a catch. There's no-one on the horizon?'

'Well I thought there was, but now I'm not so sure. A guy asked me on a date but he had to cancel to go to his grandma's funeral.'

'That's the oldest lie in the book,' Charlie said matter-of-factly.

'He said that when he got back, we would go out. I know he is back, but he hasn't called. What do you think I should do?'

'I'd call him out on it. Tell him to have the balls to just own up to changing his mind.'

'I'm not really a person that likes confrontation,' I replied, swirling the water around with my foot.

'How about you give me his number and we can call him live on air and grill him?' Charlie said, wiggling her eyebrows as her eyes twinkled maniacally.

'No. I'm really not comfortable with that idea. I might just touch base with him when I get back to clear the air.'

'Do whatever feels right for you. Personally, if it was me, I might slash his tyres or throw a paint bomb at his house,' Charlie said laughing. Who knew she was such a psycho?

'Um, I think I might just go read my book over on the sun lounges. Enjoy your swim.' I raced to put distance between Charlie and me. I tried to imagine having her castrating Sam live on air and shuddered at the thought.

I lay the generic blue and white striped resort beach towel on the sun lounge and sat back, reclining in the sun. What bliss! I then noticed that it looked like I was wearing white socks with orange streaks. The chlorine in the pool water had bleached away my fake tan, leaving me looking like a leaper. I made a mental note to only get professional tans in the future.

I opened my book but found it hard to concentrate on the words. What should I do about Sam? I didn't want to knock on his door and seem desperate. Maybe it would be best if I went back to his physio clinic and had an appointment for my ankle. It wasn't really aching too much, but I could tell him that my running was aggravating it. It was an excuse to see him and maybe he could tell me what had sent him running for the hills.

The days at the resort flew by and before I knew it, I was on the return flight home. Back to Lady Marmalade and back to my hazardous office appointments.

WAKE UP CALL

The moment I got home, I called Good Sports Physiotherapy to make an appointment to see Sam. The first available appointment was a cancellation for the next day.

I wasn't going to go in like a desperate loser. I would keep our interaction professional and hope that he had the decency to explain why he was ghosting me. I made a mental note to top up my fake tan on my feet that night so that I didn't go to the appointment looking like I was wearing albino tiger socks.

The following morning, with relatively even skin toned ankles and feet, I went to the office early to reply to all the emails I had ignored whilst soaking up the sunshine in paradise. I walked past Jason's storefront and noticed the cat's poo that had been in the shop front window had been discovered and removed. On the opposite side of the window sat a dead mangled mouse. The Kween's mini cheetah looking cat was worth its weight in gold. It only just dawned on me how apt it was for Jason to own a cheetah – they say pets take after their owners.

I flew up the stairs towards my office, just as Levi was walking down with his portfolio in hand.

'Hey Levi. Are you off to a casting?'

'Yes darling. No rest for the wicked.'

'How are the acting lessons coming along? I'm sorry I couldn't continue. It's not really my thing.'

'It's going well. I went on a date with a director for a new film who said he would definitely get me in the film as an extra, and maybe even a minor role. The days of the casting couch are still alive and well,' he said winking.

I felt a little sick in my stomach. Basically prostituting yourself for a role seemed an extreme way to get work. 'Oh,' I replied. My mind couldn't process any words of encouragement.

'I'd better run. Let's go out for a drink soon.' Levi did an air kiss next to my cheek and then turned and jogged down the stairs. I felt a tad guilty about objectifying him, but God he was a gorgeous specimen.

My office seemed a bit musty, a result of being locked up for too long. I walked over to the window to open it to let in fresh air. There on the windowsill was a dead blowfly. The last time I had seen that, I'd been paranoid that it was a bee about to sting me. Maybe if I was proactive in my own interpretation of how someone's dream might affect me, I could protect myself from this curse.

I systematically made my way through my unanswered emails, booking clients in for the next few weeks. Before I knew it, my first appointment for the day was knocking at the door.

Barton, a dreadlocked man in his forties, ambled towards the visitor chair. His eyes seemed a little bloodshot for early morning and he had a very laid-back manner about him. 'I'm so humbled to meet you. My friend Clara has so many lovely things to say about you.'

I shook Barton's hand. It was what my dad would call a wet fish handshake. His hand felt soft and limp in mine. I wasn't sure if this was his grip because I was a woman, or if he just didn't have the energy to clasp my hand any tighter. I felt almost like I was holding his hand and wobbling it about, rather than actually sharing a greeting. My mind could only wonder what he would be like in bed if his hand felt so soft and limp.

'So Barton, tell me about your dream.'

'I had this really cool dream a few weeks ago that has stayed with me. I don't normally dream, so the fact that I can remember a dream is sort of rare. I thought the universe must be trying to tell me something if it let me remember the dream.'

'Right.' I tried to keep my face neutral, when I wanted to scream at him to just tell me about the dream.

'So anyway, I was swimming in the ocean. You know I really love surfing. I once lived in Byron Bay and would surf every day.'

'Uh huh,' I replied, while my brain yelled at him to get to the point.

'Well I was out surfing, and the waves were gnarly. You know like glass barrels.'

'Right. Well, waves signify…'

Barton interrupted me, 'Hang on; I haven't got to the good part yet. I was out the back, waiting for the sets to come through and a huge whale came up alongside me. It was swimming, doing loops around me, and it was so serene. It wasn't like I was worried it was going to swallow me like in Moby Dick or anything like that. I was just in awe of being with such a majestic creature. It finally breached and flopped down next to me and I was in a shower of water. It was so amazing.'

I smiled, relieved that he had finally managed to articulate what his dream was about. 'Okay, well waves represent your emotions. It appears you are quite an emotional person. Given the waves were calm, it shows an even temperament. Whales are symbolic of strength and spirituality. Therefore, a dream of a whale in tranquil seas shows that you feel a strong association with nature and are aware of your connection with the spiritual side of life. This dream may have had a long-lasting effect on you as you were emotionally moved by the whale presented to you by your subconscious.'

Barton held his hands above his head and then flicked his hands open, gesturing that his mind was blown. 'Boom!'

I smiled, unsure of how to respond. 'So, I gather that means it resonates with you?'

'Man, you are spot on. Your insight is amazing. It's like you know me better than I know myself. Everything on this planet is interconnected, and it is so important that we care for every part of nature, I mean every animal, plant....'

I nodded along. I'd zoned out to what he was saying while trying to work out how a whale was going to impact on my life. Perhaps I could drive to a lookout to see if I could spot some whales breaching, but I wasn't sure how I would fit that into my day.

I noticed Barton looking at me strangely. I'd been sprung daydreaming and had no idea what he'd just said. 'I'm sorry, I just missed that last bit.'

'I was talking about living in the moment. Not letting life distract you from being present,' Barton said pointedly.

'Oh, I absolutely agree,' I said smiling, although I was guilty of always letting my thoughts run wild, rather than focusing on the person talking to me, or the job at hand. I made a mental note to stop letting mental notes get in the way of living in the moment.

'You know Clara is going to be over the moon when I tell her about our session today. You are amazing. Thank you for your insight.' Barton clasped his hands together into a symbol of praying and bowed in front of me. 'Namaste.' What was the correct etiquette in this situation, should I bow too, or would I look Japanese? I smiled and nodded, and mumbled, 'Thanks, you too,' before I walked around to usher him back out into the wide world.

I retrieved a voicemail that had been left whilst in session. It was from my next appointment, letting me know they had car troubles and would have to reschedule. I was a tad relieved as I was still trying to figure out how a whale was going to enter my life. With my schedule free until my physio appointment I decided I would drive to the beach to watch the waves and hopefully see a whale.

I grabbed my handbag and locked up the office. God, I loved the freedom of working for myself. What employee could just take off for the beach mid-way through a working day?

As I was walking towards the car, I could see a woman pushing a pram with her toddler sitting up taking in the world with eyes of wonder. The woman looked harried and was on the phone having a heated conversation. As they got nearer to me the angelic blond haired, brown-eyed boy threw a small plastic toy out of the pram. I retrieved the toy and to my delight saw it was a little blue whale. Crouching next to the pram, I smiled at the adorable child. It occurred to me that maybe the toy would make a squeaking sound, so I squeezed it and a jet of cold water and funky black gunk streamed out of the toy straight into my face. There it was folks, my whale encounter, water and all. I handed the toy back to the toddler and then decided that I no longer needed to visit the beach, but rather would need to go home to change my shirt that now featured an unsightly wet patch. On a positive note, the little boy burst into a fit of giggles at the sight of my whale encounter and even his mother was grinning, clearly trying to contain her laughter. At least I had provided entertainment and left them looking happier than when I first approached them.

I sat nervously in the waiting room of Good Sports Physiotherapy Clinic, unsure of the response I would get from Sam. I vowed to keep my interaction with him strictly professional. He opened the door to his treatment room and smiled as he called my name. The butterflies in my stomach were a tangled mess. I walked towards the room, hobbling slightly for effect.

'How have you been?' Sam asked as he closed the door.

'Good and you?' I replied curtly.

'Not too bad,' he replied. 'Hop up on the bed.' I'd longed to hear those words from him, but just not in this sterile setting.

'How is your ankle feeling?'

'It's much better, but it aches after I run.' He nodded, although I could tell he thought there was no possible way I would be going for runs. Little did he know my exercise regime was all based upon stalking his home.

'I would suggest low impact exercise until the ligaments are back to their normal strength. For cardio exercise I would suggest cycling, rowing or using a cross trainer until your ankle has strengthened.'

He held my foot in his strong hands and manipulated it back and forth and side to side. My brain was yelling at me to find out why he had been ignoring me and why even now he was lacking the warmth of our previous interactions. At the same time, my pride was yelling at me to keep quiet and not embarrass myself. While I was suffering this inner turmoil, my mouth just went ahead and blurted, 'Why didn't you call me when you got back? Is it because you have a girlfriend?'

Sam looked up with a curious expression and the start of a smirk. 'No.'

'Is it because you decided I'm too crazy?'

This time a full grin spread across his face. 'No.'

'Is it because you're just not that into me?' I wanted to give myself an uppercut. Why couldn't I stop my run-away mouth from humiliating me?

'No. Look now is not the time and place to have this conversation. I have another client waiting for their appointment.'

'Can we meet up tonight after you finish work?' I pleaded, sounding whiney to my own ears.

'I can't tonight. I already have plans.'

'Really?' I asked, sounding like a needy grouch.

'I am working at a soup kitchen. I go once a month.'

'Oh right,' I said, knowing a fob off when I heard it. I should have taken Charlie's advice and accepted he had changed his mind.

'You're welcome to come along. They are always looking for extra volunteers.'

I knew he expected me to balk at the idea and then he would be off scot-free, so I decided to call his bluff. 'Okay, text me the details and I'll see you there.'

He grinned. 'Great, I'll see you there.' He finally let go of my foot and I instantly missed the warmth of his hand on my flesh.

As I entered the house, Marmie pounced on me, happy to have someone to entertain her. I scooped her up to give her a cuddle just as my text message alert sounded. While others set their phone ring tones to honking horns or panic alarms, I had my phone set to a sound of wind chimes tinkling, so it felt like a little fairy was sprinkling magic to make a message appear on my phone. I fished my phone out of my pocket and saw a text from Sam with an address. Was he playing with me, sending me a bogus address, or was he genuinely going to spend his night at a soup kitchen? There was only one way to find out. I decided to change into some warm clothing. My jeans were a bit loose when I put them on. Either they had stretched or my change in diet and exercise was beginning to alter my shape. I topped up Marmie's food bowl and then gave her a quick tickle behind the ears. 'Wish me luck Marmie.'

I searched for a parking spot in the dimly lit street. Homeless people roamed past, pushing trolleys laden with their worldly belongings. What was I doing here? Was it safe for me to park my car and walk the streets in such a rough part of town? Whilst having a mental tug-o-war, a car pulled out in front of me. Surely that was a sign I should put my big girl pants on and get over myself. The address Sam had sent me seemed to be a legitimate soup kitchen, but whether he was inside still remained to be seen. Regardless of if he was there or not, it wouldn't hurt to help people less fortunate than myself.

As I walked into the sterile looking hall, the stench of unwashed bodies wafted up my nostrils. I surveyed the rows of displaced people sitting alongside each other at trestle tables. As I walked towards the kitchen, a kindly looking gentleman came over to me. 'You're new here. You can line up down that end and grab a tray.'

I knew I hadn't made an effort with my hair and makeup, but surely he didn't think I looked homeless? 'I'm actually here to help.'

'Sorry about that. You don't look like our normal customers, but I don't like to discriminate against people that turn up. If they feel they need a meal, then we are here for them. I didn't want you to feel awkward if you had reached rock bottom and needed a helping hand.'

'I completely understand. That is so lovely of you. So, what can I do to help out?'

'Well if you go and see Jan in the kitchen, she will find a job for you.'

I walked into the kitchen and located a woman wearing a name badge that proclaimed she was Jan. Within a few minutes I was at the back section of the kitchen, loading an industrial dishwasher with plates and cutlery. Jan kept coming through the kitchen with loads of dirty crockery and would take the clean lot in return. The cycle moved swiftly and before I knew it, an hour had passed. I hadn't had an opportunity to stick my head out to even see if Sam had shown up and if he was there, having been relegated to the back of the kitchen, he would have no idea that I had turned up.

I carried a stack of clean plates to the servery area and after placing them down I scanned across the sea of unwashed people to find the back of a man that could only be Sam. His broad shoulders and wavy brown hair were a dead giveaway. I watched as he crouched next to an elderly man, talking to him like an old friend. They laughed and then Sam stood, shook the man's hand and then walked to another person, collecting used plates as he went.

My heart fluttered as I realised this soup kitchen wasn't an elaborate ruse he had set up to get out of seeing me tonight. Sam truly was a saint and deserved better than someone as flaky as me. Sam turned to walk back to the kitchen, and we locked eyes. A huge grin spread across his face and his eyes lit up. I gave him a little wave and then walked back out to tackle the leaning tower of dirty plates that had accumulated near the dishwasher.

Slowly the rate of dirty dishes dropped. I wiped sweat from my brow. Who knew being a dish pig was such hot work? Jan carried in a few odd plates. 'Darling, thank you so much for your help tonight. You were a godsend. I think you've probably done enough for one day. I'll finish off these last plates. Why don't you get going?'

'Okay, thanks. By the way Jan, you guys do an amazing job here.'

'We try to,' Jan replied, smiling.

I gathered my handbag and walked out into the hall that was practically empty. I watched Sam stacking chairs in the corner. I wasn't leaving without speaking with him, so I sat down next to a scruffy looking woman to wait.

'How was your meal tonight?' I asked. Small talk had never really been my forte.

'Not too bad. I'm Elspeth,' she said with a slight Scottish brogue. She reached out to shake my hand, and I noticed dirt ingrained in her skin and lodged deep under her nails.

I shook her hand. 'It's nice to meet you. I'm Maggie.'

'Are ye Scottish, with a name like Maggie?'

'No, I was born and bred here in Australia.'

'Oh. So, what are you doing here Maggie?' Elspeth asked as she slurped on her soup.

'I'm just here to give a helping hand.'

'You people are incredible. You know I was living rough for a few weeks before I found out about this place. Thought I was going to die of hunger, if I didn't get murdered by my ex first.'

'I'm so sorry to hear that. Are you still living on the streets?'

'Aye, but I've got a bed in the local hostel tonight, which is why I was so late in getting here for dinner.' She hungrily stuffed a chunk of bread into her mouth.

'Where do you normally hang out during the day? I've got some clothes that I'm about to get rid of. I could drop them off to you if you'd like.'

'That'd be great. You can usually find me in the park in the centre of town.'

I looked down at her feet. She was wearing joggers with a hole ripped in the side.

'What size shoes do you wear?'

'I'm a size seven. Shoes are a funny thing, aren't

they? You can never really know what size shoes fit as they seem to change from brand to brand.'

I wore size nine shoes, so they would be way too big, but I made a mental note to go buy her some warm enclosed shoes from a local department store.

Out of the corner of my eye I could see that Sam had stopped stacking chairs and was leaning against a wall watching my interaction with Elspeth.

'I have to go, but I'll see you again soon with those clothes okay.'

Elspeth reached out her hand to clasp my wrist. 'Thank you, luv.'

Sam's face lit up as I walked towards him. 'So, you made it.'

'Yep, I'm now a fully fledged dish pig,' I said, smiling proudly at my effort.

'I'm sure Jan was grateful for the help.'

'So, you really do help out here once a month?'

'Yep. I started when I was in high school as a community service project. It feels good to give back to the community. Not everyone is as lucky as us.'

I nodded. Of course, I had always known these places existed, but I'd never really given any thought to being involved. This small exposure had shown me how impactful just a few hours of help could be. I vowed to myself to commit to helping out on a regular basis.

'If you're free, do you want to go grab a bite to eat? There's a quiet pub around the corner,' Sam said.

'That would be nice.'

Sam led me to a nearby pub that smelt of stale beer and fried food. We walked to a clear table and as I went to sit down, Sam came and possessively took hold of the back of the chair.

'Oh, sorry. You sit there, I can sit on the other side.'

Sam laughed. 'I'm holding the chair out for you.'

I stared at him dumbfounded. Did guys really do that in real life? I'd only ever seen that type of behaviour in black and white movies.

'You know you don't have to do that.'

'My mum would kill me if she thought I wasn't

gentlemanly.'

'Well, I don't want your mum to have murder on her conscience,' I said as I sat in the chair.

Sam shook his head and laughed as he took his seat.

'How was your trip to Fiji?' I asked.

'It was okay,' Sam said noncommittally.

'The funeral went well?'

'Yes. I think my grandmother would have liked it and it was nice to see my family.'

There was a deafening silence. I wasn't going to play the whining love interest again and so apart from asking why he was ghosting me, I had nothing to talk about. At this point, I just hoped we could salvage a friendship. I reached for the menu.

Sam took a deep breath. 'I should apologise for not contacting you when I got back. I've had a lot on my mind.'

'Sam, I'm not wanting to complicate your life. You know you can talk to me, right?'

Sam nodded. 'You see, when I was back in Fiji, my mum asked if I would consider moving back home. She offered me a treatment room in her medical practice.'

'Right.'

'I was also contacted by the Fijian Rugby Union Coach about joining them as their trainer and physio for the Fijian Olympic team.'

'Wow, that's an impressive gig.'

'Yes. I never made it to the Olympics, so it would fulfill that dream to some extent.'

'So, when do you move?' I asked, trying to keep my face neutral.

'I haven't decided what to do yet. That's why I didn't contact you. I didn't want to lead you on if I'm going to then walk away.'

'I understand,' I said.

'These are great opportunities, but on the other hand, I have an established practice which is doing really well, and I've just met you. I'm really torn.'

'Won't your mum be heartbroken if you don't go home?'

'My mum wants me to be happy. There's no pressure from her, it was just an offer to consider. The thing is that she has a busy life with her work and my half-brothers and stepdad. I could go back to Fiji, but it won't necessarily feel like I'm going home.'

'Is there a chance you could accept the Olympic gig, without living in Fiji?'

'I hadn't really thought about that. I guess I could ask.'

'I really enjoy your company, but I wouldn't ever want to get in the way of you achieving your dreams. Sam, you need to follow your heart and do what is right for you. I'd like it if we can be friends and you don't have to worry about my feelings if you decide to move. I'll be cool with that, if it's what you want.' I wouldn't really be cool with it, but he didn't need to know I'd be devastated if he moved.

'Thanks for your support. Maybe my dreams will reveal what I should do.'

'You know I'm always happy to decipher your dreams. As long as they don't involve death and torture.'

'So are people's dreams still being transferred into your life?'

'Yep. I had a whale encounter today!'

'Wait, what?'

'My client had a dream about a whale. Thankfully I came across a toy whale.'

'Oh, I thought you must have been out in the ocean today. It's a bit chilly to be swimming at this time of year.'

'It's equally chilly to have some kid's skanky bath water squirt all over you.'

Sam burst into laughter. 'That would only happen to you.'

I nodded. 'I know. I need to work out how to stop these dreams becoming my reality.'

A waitress came over, interrupting our conversation. 'Are you ready to order?'

I gazed at the menu in my hands. 'Umm, I'll have a chicken schnitzel please.'

'Make it two,' Sam said, handing back the menus.

'So, while I was away I was thinking about the mysterious cat dumper. How old is Lady Marmalade?'

'She is close to seven weeks old.'

'I was thinking that people sell kittens when they are weaned from their mother, around eight weeks of age. Instead of looking for purple bin liners, we should be looking for litters of kittens for sale.'

My first thought was that Sam had said 'we' and not 'you.' He was treating us as a team. My heart fluttered a little. My next thought was that it was such an obvious solution. I was shocked I hadn't thought of it myself.

'If you narrowed your search area to this local community, there can't be that many people selling kittens.'

'You're not just a pretty face,' I said smiling at Sam. I quickly typed 'ginger kitten for sale' into the browser for Gumtree and eBay in our local area. There were no hits.

'Maybe the reason they dumped Lady Marmalade is that she is ginger and they thought she wouldn't sell.'

I removed the word 'ginger' from my browser search and ten ads appeared. It was too late to contact any of the sellers tonight, so I decided to start my investigation in the morning.

The waitress suddenly materialized, placing our meals in front of us. I had a newfound respect for hospitality staff after my night's work at the soup kitchen. I would normally not have acknowledged her with more than a grunt, but instead I looked her in the eyes. 'Thank you. It looks delicious and your service has been excellent.'

She looked at me to check if I was being sarcastic and then seeing I was genuine, she blushed and smiled. 'Thanks. I hope you enjoy your meal.'

She turned to Sam. 'My workmate Trev asked me to ask you if you are Sam Telavatu?'

Sam grinned, being obviously used to being asked this question. 'Yes, I am.'

'Would you mind if Trev got a photo with you? I mean, after you finish your dinner.'

Sam smiled graciously. 'Sure, that's fine.'

I looked over to the waitress relaying her conversation to the guy behind the bar who was grinning like a Cheshire cat.

No sooner had I finished the last mouthful of my dinner than my plate was whisked away and Trev the barman approached.

Sam stood and shook his hand.

'I knew it was you! Sam Telavatu, the legend of Fiji. That try you scored in the dying minutes of that match at the 2011 World Cup will go down in history as being textbook perfect. I coach my kid's team and I show them that try as inspiration. It was such a pity you had to retire due to injury.' I couldn't believe how much this guy knew about Sam. He was a walking Wikipedia page for him.

'Thanks, man. It was devastating to have to retire when I blew my knee but that's professional sport for you.'

'Can I get a pic with you? My son won't believe it.' Trev the barman was practically hopping on the spot with excitement. He handed me his phone, and I took a photo of the two of them embracing like long-lost friends.

'So great to meet you mate,' Trev said, shaking Sam's hand vigourously.

'You too,' Sam replied, trying to extricate his hand.

As we walked back to my car, I noticed Sam was walking on the road side of me. Amused by his chivalrous ways, I dropped back, under the guise of tying my shoelace. When I stood up again, I walked to the road side of the path. He discreetly slowed down his pace and then suddenly walked up alongside me again on the road side once more. I laughed. 'You passed the test. You really are such a gentleman,' I said with a curtsey, holding out my hands to the side to mime holding a skirt.

Playing along, he dipped his imaginary hat. 'Thank you, ma'am.'

When my car came into sight, my brain went into overdrive. Was he going to kiss me? Should I try to kiss him? Were we just friends? Were we more than friends? Should I invite him home to my place? The questions were firing one after the other, making it hard to concentrate on what Sam was saying.

As we walked alongside my car, he reached down and kissed the back of my hand while bowing, continuing the earlier charade of chivalry. He'd taken the safe option and while I wanted nothing more than to kiss him on the lips, I instead did the honorable thing and respected his decision to stay in the friend zone.

CRAZY DAYS

My planned workload for the day was pretty light. I had a radio session first thing, then a few hours break where I had planned to do bookwork and then a client session in the afternoon. While I was desperate to start making enquiries about the people selling kittens, my first priority was to put together a care pack for Elspeth.

As soon as I hung up the phone after doing my radio spot, I began pilfering through my wardrobe, looking for warm clothes that would be appropriate for someone living on the streets. Within half an hour I had filled a garbage bag full of clothes. It seemed wrong to be hoarding these clothes when less fortunate people really needed them. If Elspeth didn't want all the clothes, I'm sure she would know people who would gladly use them.

I then drove to the local shopping centre. Grabbing a trolley, I threw in items with glee. I located a new pair of runners in size 7, together with a pair of boots, three pairs of socks, a warm blanket, hand sanitizer, deodorant, a towel, a trashy magazine and a family size block of chocolate, because, well, everyone knows chocolate makes people happy. I then bought a backpack and shoved all the items in, ready to hand them over to Elspeth.

I drove to the park and grabbed the items for Elspeth. Wandering around, I was dismayed to see so many homeless people. I knew I shouldn't be shocked because the previous night I had seen firsthand the number of people being served at the soup kitchen, but it seemed harder to accept actually seeing them living rough.

Some looked off into the middle distance, mumbling to themselves, while others crouched, reading a newspaper they must have found discarded in a bin. I eventually located Elspeth by the base of a tree, huddled in a ball hugging her knees to her chest.

'Elspeth?'

Elspeth raised her head to look at me warily. She was sporting a black eye that hadn't been there the night before.

'What happened to you? Are you all right? Should I take you to the hospital?'

'I'll be fine. It's not the first time, nor will it be the last.'

'What happened?' I asked, feeling sick in my stomach.

'My ex found me. He knew the pension came out yesterday. Asked for my money. When I dinna hand it over he punched me right in my face, then stole the money from my purse.'

'You have to go to the police.'

'It's no use. They aint gonna do nothin 'bout anything. We are both just street vermin.'

'No one deserves to live like this.'

'I've made my choices in life. No use crying over spilt milk.'

I could feel tears threatening to spill out of my eyes.

'I brought you some things,' I said, lamely handing her the backpack and garbage bag of clothes.

This time tears flowed freely down Elspeth's cheeks, leaving a trail of clean skin in their wake. 'Oh macushla. You give me hope that there are still good people in this world.'

I couldn't speak. Tears streamed down my cheeks. Here was a woman who had a tough shell from years of abuse, but my small kindness had brought her to tears. There had to be a way to find her a safe home in which to live. I made a silent vow to find permanent housing for her.

Her face lit up when she discovered the magazine and chocolate. 'Oh, wee Maggie, you know the way to my heart.'

I sank to the ground next to Elspeth and wrapped her in a hug. 'I want you to listen to me. You don't have to live this way. I can try to help you.'

'I'm a lost cause.'

'No one is ever a lost cause. Do you think I deserve to be bashed and robbed?'

Elspeth looked at me horrified. 'No, of course not.'

'That's right and neither do you!'

'But I've done things in my life that I shouldna done. I have made bad choices.'

'That might be the case, but that doesn't define you.'

'That's fine for you to say but look at you.

You're a pretty young girl with her whole life ahead of her. I'm a stinky old homeless woman. People avert their eyes when they walk past me. They dinna want to look at me, in case they catch my desperation.'

I nodded. I'd been guilty of that in the past. It was easier to pretend homeless people were invisible than run the risk of them begging from you.

'No one wants to give me a job and without a job I can't afford a home and without a home I'm at the mercy of every mongrel out here.'

'Do you have any skills?'

'I worked in a factory once, packing items on an assembly line. I also worked as a maid in a hotel a few years ago.'

'Okay, so you have work experience. You have skills to offer an employer.'

'I guess.'

'You now have toiletries and clean fresh clothes. If you believe in yourself, then others will start to believe in you. You've got to fake it, til you make it.'

'Maybe, but no-one's gonna be able to look at

me with a big fat black eye.'

'Okay. The first thing we need to do is get you to hospital. If you have a fractured eye socket, it could require surgery. If nothing else, they can give you a bed and some painkillers. Come with me.'

'Oh, I don't know. I don't wanna be a nuisance.'

'Hospitals are there to treat sick and injured people. You're not being a nuisance if you are sick or injured. I'm not taking no for an answer.'

'But where can I put my things?'

I hadn't considered the storage of her supermarket trolley of possessions.

'Let me check something.' I turned away from Elspeth and rang Sam.

'Hi Sam. I'm at the park with a lady from the soup kitchen last night. She's been assaulted and I'm going to take her to hospital. Do you know if the soup kitchen could store her possessions for a while?'

'I don't think it's open at this time of day. There is a nearby hostel. They don't usually let people store their things, but they might bend their rules given the circumstances. I'll text you their number.'

'Thanks Sam. I'll let you know how it goes.'

No sooner had I hung up than the phone tinkled its wind chime magic ringtone with a message from Sam.

I immediately rang the hostel and, after explaining the situation, they agreed to store Elspeth's trolley until she was out of hospital.

'Elspeth, I've arranged storage for your trolley. Come with me. You can wait in my car while I wheel your trolley over to the hostel.'

'I swear you are an angel from heaven.'

Elspeth gathered up her new backpack and garbage bag of clothes and I pushed the trolley.

I zig-zagged my way to the car. I'm sure anyone who saw me would have thought I'd had a morning cocktail or ten. Once Elspeth was safely locked in my car, I tried to maneuver the trolley the few city blocks to the hostel. I wondered whether it was in the manufacturing agreement for all trolley makers to include one wheel that refused to turn and one that spun wildly doing nothing. They probably had assembly lines where people checked on quality control. If the trolley refused to move in a straight line, then it was good to be released to the world.

I'd worked up a sweat by the time I reached the

hostel. Thankfully the lady I had spoken to on the phone greeted me at the door to the hostel and she took over trying to guide the uncontrollable trolley.

By the time I reached the car, I could see Elspeth sitting in the front seat of the car shaking.

I whipped the passenger door open. 'Are you okay Elspeth? Are you epileptic?'

With her head in her hands she replied, 'No. I'm just having a panic attack. I have chronic anxiety. I don't think I can go to the hospital.'

I thought back to my days of university training. I took hold of Elspeth's hands and clasped them in mine. In a calm and clinical voice, I said, 'Just take some deep breaths. I want you to breathe in for six seconds, hold it for six seconds and breathe out for six seconds.'

Elspeth followed my instructions and within a few minutes her breathing had started to slow and regulate.

'I want you to know that the staff at the hospital are there to help you. I will stay with you as long as they will let me. Your health is important. Elspeth, look at me.' She raised her pale blue eyes. 'You are important.'

She nodded and gave me a half-hearted smile. I could see that she didn't truly believe my statement, but I was going to make it my mission to get her to realise that people did care about her. That she truly was important.

Seeing the state of Elspeth's injuries when we arrived at the emergency department, the triage nurse ushered Elspeth directly into a curtained off section. It warmed my heart that the nurse recognised the importance of trying to keep Elspeth's humility protected.

I sat beside Elspeth while we waited for the doctor to come to inspect her injuries.

'So, tell me what brought you to Australia.'

'I had an abusive, alcoholic father in Scotland. When I was ten, my mammy decided we should leave, so she found a charity that agreed to pay the fare for her and her six kids to go to Australia. We only had the clothes on our backs. My little sister got a disease, um, something fever.' She stopped to try to recall the illness.

'Yellow fever?'

'No.'

'Glandular fever?'

'No, that's not it.'

'Saturday Night fever?' I joked.

Elspeth burst into hysterical laughing with tears rolling down her face. 'I'm pretty sure that wasn't it.'

'Scarlet fever?'

'That's the one. Well little Ainsley was only two. She was covered head to toe in this red rash. Within a week, the sore throat she started with turned into pneumonia. You could hear the liquid in her lungs when she breathed. Mammy wouldn't let us other kids go near her for fear that we would catch it too. Little Ainsley ended up dying when we were out to sea.'

'Oh. I'm so sorry. How tragic for you.'

'I often think about what Ainsley would be doing with her life now, had she made it. Then again, she missed out on living a tough life, so maybe she was the lucky one.'

It broke my heart to hear Elspeth's lifelong suffering.

'Where did you live when your family first

arrived in Australia?'

'Mammy got a job as a maid in a hotel in Goulburn. The deal included a room that she and us five kids could share.'

'I only went to school for three years in Australia. By the time I was thirteen I was working in the hotel as a maid too. It meant we got another room to help us spread out a bit as it was very cramped, us all living in one room for three years.'

'That is an amazing sacrifice you made for your family.'

'By sixteen, I was drinking after work every day. Mammy had begun a relationship with the hotelier, so he moved in with her and all the kids moved in with me. He was an abusive man, but Mam didn't dare stand up against him because then we'd all be kicked out on the streets. Living in a cramped room with my four brothers was tough. They would always be sparring with each other. My brother Robbie called it rough housing, but I think it was actually just the way they thought men behaved. It was nothing for them to be punching each other with closed fists – you'd think they were mortal enemies, but it was their way of bonding. I remember once, a kid gave one of my brothers a hard time. Within half an hour my other brothers had beaten the living daylights out of the poor boy.

'One afternoon, the hotelier said if I was open to making more money by "spending alone time" with some of his customers he would give me another room, so I agreed. I started in the oldest profession known to man at age sixteen.'

Tears rolled silently down my cheeks. My heart ached for the sixteen-year-old Elspeth. She'd had such a tragic life. No wonder she expected the worst out of everyone.

Our conversation was cut short as the registrar, a large bear of a man, came into the room. I watched as Elspeth shrunk in front of my eyes. She looked scared and withdrawn, casting her eyes downward.

'Tell me what's happened,' he said gruffly.

'My ex beat me up,' Elspeth replied meekly.

'Uh huh. Any dizziness, double vision or headaches?' I looked at him incredulously. Of course, her bloody head ached – her face was black and blue.

'I have a headache and I'm not sure about my vision. I don't have very good vision at the best of times.'

I interrupted. 'Do you have prescription glasses I can fetch for you?'

'I've never been able to afford glasses luv. I just make do,' Elspeth replied.

The doctor scribbled some notes on a chart. 'Someone will be here to see you to do some tests soon.'

As he left the room, he neglected to pull the curtain closed behind him. I stood to draw the curtain in order to give Elspeth some privacy and saw Sophie, one of my university classmates, walking the halls.

'Soph,' I called out.

'Oh my God, Maggie, how are you?'

'I'm good. How about you?' Sophie looked exhausted, presumably from her time working in the hospital.

'I'm good. I'm in my second year as a psychology registrar here at the hospital. I'll be fully qualified in six months. What are you doing here? Is everything okay?'

I nodded. 'Yes. I've just brought in a homeless lady who was assaulted.' I moved closer, lowering my voice. 'Actually Soph, do you think there is any way you can make the hospital keep her in here for a few days so I can help arrange some accommodation for her?'

Sophie grimaced. 'I'm not sure that I'll have much sway. Does she suffer from any psychological issues?'

'Yes. She's definitely got issues with chronic anxiety and I think also PTSD. Is that enough to keep her in for further examinations?'

'Did you say she is suicidal?' Sophie said nodding her head at me.

Realising this was the only way for her to be admitted I nodded. 'Yep. Sure is.'

'Then we will definitely have to keep her in for a few days for assessment.'

I leaned over and whispered to Sophie, 'Thank you.'

'I have to run but let's catch up soon for a coffee. I hear you on the radio all the time. Maybe you can tell me if my dreams will come true.'

'Sounds good. Thanks Soph.'

As I pulled back the curtain to Elspeth's bed, she cowered in fear.

'It's just me.'

Elspeth relaxed and pulled the cotton waffle weave blanket up under her chin.

I leaned over to whisper in her ear. 'Elspeth, I just bumped into a friend. She said if you said you were feeling suicidal, they would keep you in here for a few days. That will give me some time to see if I can find you some permanent accommodation.'

She nodded. 'You're a bonny lass. It's not as if I haven't thought about ending things over the years. My brother Donny committed suicide when he was twenty-five.'

'My heart breaks for you.'

'It was only a few weeks after my brother Robbie died of a drug overdose. Donny couldn't imagine life without his brother.'

'Have you ever had any counseling for the grief and trauma you've encountered in your life?'

'Oh, everyone has to die at some time.'

'How did your mum cope with losing three of her kids at such a young age?'

'Mam drowned her sorrows in the bottom of a bottle. It dinna help that she lived in a pub. She died of cirrhosis of the liver in her sixties.'

'Are you in contact with your other two brothers?'

Elspeth shook her head. 'Last I heard Connor had moved back to Scotland and I dinna know where Lachlan ended up. He left home when he was eighteen and none of us have heard from him since. I like to imagine he is the CEO of some company, living the high life, married with a brood of his own kids. I sort of don't want to know what he is doing with his life, because it might ruin the illusion I've built in my mind.'

It only just dawned on me that Elspeth was truly alone. She had no family support, and it seemed her only friends were transient displaced homeless people.

I clasped Elspeth's hand in mine. 'I want you to know that I'm going to do all that I can to help you get your life back on track. The first step is to get you off the streets and then find you a job. When they do a psych assessment, apart from telling them you're suicidal, please tell them about the grief you've suffered in your life. Your mental health is as important as your physical health.'

'I've never really thought about it that way.'

'I have a graduate diploma in psychology. You will have seen, firsthand living on the streets, how someone's mental health can affect their whole life.'

The curtain drew back again, and I watched as Elspeth automatically stiffened with fear. Sophie entered the room and walked over to Elspeth.

'I'm Sophie, the psychology registrar.' She reached out to shake Elspeth's hand. I could see that such a small token of humanity touched Elspeth.

'I believe you have had some thoughts of harming yourself.' She nodded at Elspeth to encourage her to agree.

Elspeth looked at me and winked. 'Yes.' Thankfully Sophie was my friend, as had it been any other doctor, they would have questioned Elspeth's sincerity.

As Sophie filled in the chart she asked, 'Do you suffer from any known mental health issues?'

'No.'

I interrupted, 'Elspeth, what about your anxiety? You had a panic attack before we came here.'

'Is that anxiety? I've never given it a name before. I thought that everyone has times like that.'

'And I think you also have PTSD. Every time that curtain opens you cower with fear. I think it is linked to the physical abuse you have encountered your whole life.'

Sophie nodded, writing furiously on the chart.

'Okay Elspeth; the ED registrar has recommended a head CT scan to see if there are any fractures. After you have been assessed for your physical injuries, we will transfer you to the psych ward for a few days.'

An alarm on my phone beeped, reminding me of my next work appointment.

'Elspeth, I'm sorry but I have to go back to work now. I'll come back to see you again tonight.'

I looked over towards Sophie. 'Thanks for everything Soph. I'll see you soon.'

'Take care,' Sophie said as she finished marking up Elspeth's chart.

Driving back to work I called Sam, but it diverted immediately to voicemail. 'Hi Sam, it's me. I mean Maggie. You know, your neighbour and fellow soup kitchen volunteer. Anyway I'm just heading to work for a session with a client, but when you get a chance after 3pm, can you please call me back? I'm just wondering if you know anyone I can contact to help find some permanent accommodation for Elspeth. Thanks. Bye. Speak to you soon. Okay. Bye. I'm going to hang up now. Bye.' I hung up and groaned. How was it possible to sound so inarticulate in a message? I just wished I could erase that voice message and record another one, but instead I would have to just live with the fact that Sam would hear me sounding like a blathering idiot.

My mind was racing with options for Elspeth as I walked up the stairs to my office. Just as I put the keys in the door an echoed voice called out, 'Is that you Maggie?'

I looked around but couldn't see where the voice was coming from, so I called out into the void, 'Yes.'

A sound, reminiscent of a herd of elephants stampeding, rang through the stairwell. Suddenly Levi appeared. 'I've been waiting to see you all day.'

As much as there was once a time I would have melted to hear those words, I was wary about what Levi wanted. 'Oh, really.'

'Darling, I have a client wanting a "plus sized model" for a photo shoot. Can you do it?'

'I'm hardly a model,' I laughed.

'I sort of already sent them a photo of you and they said your dark hair and green eyes were mesmerizing.'

I shook my head, unsure that I had heard correctly. 'Sorry, you already sent them a photo of me?' Why on earth did Levi have a photo of me? He must have been stalking my Instagram as much I had his.

'Yes. I'm sorry babe. I know I should have asked you first, but I thought I'd check if you had the look they were after before I bothered you.'

I'd never been good at rejecting people who were asking for favours.

'When is it and what would I have to do?'

'It's in two weeks. It's a three-hour shoot in a studio. What size do you wear?' Isn't it an unwritten rule that people shouldn't talk about religion, politics or clothes sizes? I wondered if I should lie and say I'm a size twelve, then not fit in the clothes, or confess to the perfectly sculpted model that I actually wore a size fourteen? I took a deep breath. I guess it didn't matter to Levi what size I was, as he would never be attracted to me.

'I'm a fourteen,' I mumbled.

'Perfect. I'll send you a message with the deets. Ciao Bella,' Levi said, running back up the stairs to his office.

How on earth did I just get steamrolled into doing a photo shoot? Kayleigh would wet herself with laughter when she heard about it.

I opened my computer and while I waited for my next appointment, I reviewed the list of people selling kittens. I only had a short window of opportunity to try to discover the identity of the kitten dumper. I pulled up the first ad which was for pedigreed Siamese kittens. I googled a bit of information about them, trying to decipher if Marmie could have been part of that litter, but to be pedigreed, both the parents would have been Siamese and they couldn't possibly have given birth to my little ginger friend.

I scrolled to the next ad. There was little detail. It just read, 'Litter of kittens. Fully immunized. Ready to go to new home in next two weeks.' The timing was right. I called and made an appointment to visit the following day.

A knock on the door pulled my attention away from the computer. Honestly, I felt I was being tugged in a million directions at the moment. I was trying to be a superhero, fighting for the rights of abandoned cats and people, while helping the community understand their subconscious in their dreams and as of half an hour ago, also being a part-time model. Could my life get any weirder?

I smiled and ushered my new client to the desk.

'Hi Scott. Welcome. Please take a seat.'

'Thanks,' Scott replied as he straddled the seat.

'What brought you here today?'

'Me missus booked me in. I told her about a dream I had the other day and she said I had to find out what it meant.'

'Okay. Well how about you share your dream with me?' I poised my pen over my notebook.

'I was out in the wild, camping near a stream. It was really serene. I was catching fish and grilling them over an open fire. The next thing a huge brown bear appeared out of nowhere. I couldn't run, even though I was trying desperately to escape. It hurtled over to me. I tried to fend it off with sticks but it broke them and slashed at my face. I then ended up wrestling with the bear. Finally it went to maul my face, and I woke up screaming. My whole body was covered in sweat. I got the impression that it might have killed me.' Shivers ran down my spine. I'd forgotten to give him the disclaimer that he couldn't tell me dreams where someone is injured or killed. A lump formed in my throat and I tried to gather my thoughts to respond.

'Bears are symbolic of strength, power and independence. You seem like an independent person given you were camping alone in the wilderness in your dream. The fact that you took on fighting an aggressive bear also reinforces the fact that you consider yourself powerful. This dream really highlights that you are a tenacious person. If you are encountering any problems in your life, you know that you have the ability to deal with them independently. What do you do for a job?'

'I'm a builder.'

'Do you have staff?'

'Nah. They're too much hassle. If you want a job done right, you have to do it yourself.'

'There's that independence and self-assuredness. You know that you have the skills to back yourself in any situation.'

'Yeah, I guess I do.'

'This dream wasn't about making you feel weak and fearful. It was actually quite the opposite.'

'That's good to know.'

'It is also said that dreams about bears are good luck.'

'Cool. I'm waiting to hear on a big tender. Maybe I'll get the job.'

'I think there is a very good chance that you might. You definitely seem very capable.'

Scott continued to talk about the specs of the tender, but I struggled to focus, as all I could think about was how this dream was going to affect my life. I was scared to leave the office in case a bear mauled me. Maybe the myths of drop bears that kids used to tell back in school were real and I would find myself ambushed walking below a gum tree.

After Scott left the office, I tried to distract myself from his ominous dream. I only had to worry about obscure threats. Poor Elspeth was living under constant threat all day every day. I Googled housing assistance, but skimming the pages of information from the government, it looked like there was a lot of red tape to get considered for housing. The phone rang, and I was relieved to see it was Sam returning my call.

'Hello neighbour and fellow soup kitchen volunteer,' he said.

I cringed as I recalled my message to him.

'Thanks for calling me back. I was wondering if you know someone who can help Elspeth get housing? I know it's a long shot, but I figured if you've been volunteering at the soup kitchen for years, you might know someone.'

'I used to be the ambassador for a domestic violence charity. I could call them to find out if they can help.'

'I forget you were a big-time sports star. That would be great if you don't mind calling them.'

'Anything for you.'

My heart lurched. Sam was always sending me such mixed signals. Was he into me or was he just this charming with everyone?

'When you say you'd do anything for me, does that include fighting off a brown bear trying to kill me?'

Sam laughed. 'What?'

'My last client had a dream a bear mauled him

and now I'm scared about what is going to happen to me.'

Sam was silent a moment. 'Stay there. I'll be over soon.'

'As my body guard?'

'You'll see.'

Within twenty minutes there was a knock on my office door. I walked over to open the door and a teddy bear was thrust through the gap, mauling or maybe snuggling into the crook of my neck. I shrieked with fright.

Sam pushed the door open. 'Problem solved,' he said laughing.

'Oh my god Sam, I almost peed myself.'

Sam wrapped me in a hug. 'I'm sorry if I scared you. I was just trying to circumvent you getting mauled by a real bear. There is a circus in town you know.'

With my arms wrapped around his muscly back and being inside his bear hug, the thought of a bear was no longer frightening.

He pulled free and sat down.

'Where did you find a teddy bear at such short notice?'

'It's from the toy box in our waiting room. It's there to keep little kids amused.'

I looked at the teddy bear I had been hugging to my chest. It had a strange crusty substance stuck to the fur, either remnants of biscuit or possibly dried boogers. I dropped the teddy bear into Sam's lap.

'On the way here I called that charity. They said that they are re-homing someone in a week and Elspeth could take her room.'

'That's amazing news Sam. Wait until Elspeth hears. You truly are a saint.'

He smiled and his whole face lit up. 'Maybe you're the saint. You are the one trying to find her a home. Without you she wouldn't have even sought medical assistance today.'

Maybe I was the Mother Teresa to his Gandhi.

'I made an appointment to check out some kittens at 9am tomorrow morning if you are free.'

'I'm not doing my Saturday clinic this week so I'm happy to come with you, just in case they are the kitten dumpers. I don't want you to be in danger.'

'Honestly, I think the only danger I might be in is if the kittens are too cute and I decide to adopt them all.'

'Well then I'll be there to save you from yourself.'

'Okay it's a date.'

'I've got to get back to work. I have a few late appointments tonight. I'll come to your place in the morning around 8.30am.'

I nodded, while my inner voice was yelling to invite him to stay the night so he didn't have to get up early in the morning. My common sense won out when I realised there wouldn't be much of a time saving as he only lived a few doors away.

'Thanks for coming to my rescue today.' I gave Sam a brief hug, unsure of the correct etiquette to use to say goodbye to someone you were into but you weren't sure if they were into you.

I arrived at the hospital and went to the reception to find out to which room Elspeth had been relocated. The woman at the desk typed on the computer and came back at me with a blank expression. 'Sorry, no one here by that name.'

'I think she was being moved to the psych ward. Can you check there please?' I waited while she typed again.

'No, I'm sorry.'

'But I left her here earlier this afternoon. She can't just disappear into thin air.'

The receptionist began typing again. 'Oh, she was admitted to psych this afternoon, but she checked herself out at 5.15pm.'

'What? Why didn't you stop her?'

'She wasn't committed, she was there of her own free will.'

'Is Doctor Sophie White still working?'

The receptionist typed away again.

'No, I'm sorry. Her shift ended at 3pm.'

I racked my brain trying to think where Elspeth would be.

I drove directly to the soup kitchen to see if she had gone there to eat, but even though it was as busy as the previous night, Elspeth was nowhere to be seen. I then drove to the hostel, because surely she would have returned to retrieve her belongings and maybe a bed for the night.

The lady that had greeted me early in the day was at the reception. Before I even opened my mouth to speak she spoke, as if reading my mind. 'If you're looking for Elspeth, she's come and been. We didn't have any spare beds, so she is out there sleeping rough tonight.'

This was the worst-case scenario I had envisioned. I drove down to the park and even though a few nights earlier I wouldn't have dared to walk alone in this area, my need to find Elspeth took precedence over my fear. I'd read an article once that suggested women could use their car keys like a weapon, lodging them between their fingers to resemble a lame version of Wolverine. My key was one where the metal part flipped inside the plastic molded casing. I flicked open the key, sure that if it came to using my key as a weapon it would collapse back inside the casing at the first sign of any pressure. Examining the key, I also noticed the end was square. Seriously, how was a girl supposed to use this as self-defense when it didn't even have a pointy end to stab someone with it? Maybe because the end was a blunt square, any damage it caused might be considered a blunt force injury. I giggled at my silly musings as I walked through the park.

As I neared the tree where I had found Elspeth earlier the morning, I could see a figure hidden beneath blankets.

I crouched down next to the person. 'Elspeth?'

Elspeth poked her head out of the blanket. 'Hello luv.'

'What are you doing here?'

'It's where I live.'

'But you were going to stay at the hospital for a few nights. I made sure they would transfer you to the psych ward and keep you for a few days.'

'That place was full of crazies. If they weren't screaming, they were crying or lying around like corpses. I'd rather deal with the crazies out here than spend another minute in that ward.'

'What did the hospital say about your injury?'

'You know I thought you had to be smart to be a doctor, but I'm not so sure. They said I have a hairline fracture that they can't do anything for, but they gave me a script for antibiotics. They know that I was in the hospital because I'd been assaulted and he stole all my money. How do they expect I'm going to be able to pay to get the script filled?' She laughed sardonically.

The blanket slipped down and I could see she was nursing a brown paper bag.

'Where did you get the drink?' I asked, not understanding how she could somehow afford to buy alcohol but not medication.

'A kind social worker at the hospital gave me twenty dollars for transport.' She raised her bottle high in the air. 'This is really the only medication I need. It works as a painkiller, warms my blood, lets me forget about life and helps me sleep. It's a magic potion I tell you.'

'You can't stay here Elspeth. It's not safe.' I wracked my brain for any possible solution and the only thing I could come up with was to bring her home to my place. Maybe I could trust her to stay and it wasn't as if I had anything worth stealing. I took a deep breath and hoped I wouldn't regret my decision. 'Why don't you come home and stay at my place for a few nights? A friend of mine has found somewhere you can live permanently in about a week's time. In the meantime you can sleep on my couch.'

'Thank you luv, but that's too much of an imposition. You've already done so much for me.'

'I insist. It's only for a week. Come on; get your things, you're coming home with me.'

We unloaded Elspeth's trolley full of items into the boot of my car and abandoned the trolley by the side of the road. We hadn't even reached the end of the street when I saw in the rear-view mirror, some man zig-zagging his way along the pathway, having already claimed the wonky trolley as his own.

PLAYING CAT AND MOUSE

The moment Elspeth entered my home, Lady Marmalade rubbed herself against her legs, whilst ignoring my existence. I'd never really understood how fickle cats could be.

Elspeth was delighted by the attention. Having never seemingly been shown much love in her life, Elspeth lapped up Marmie's unadulterated adoration. I left most of Elspeth's stinky swag in the car and then ushered her into the shower, handing her fresh toiletries, a towel and clean clothes. I was shocked that the hospital hadn't let her shower while she was in their care.

When Elspeth returned from the shower she looked years younger. All the ingrained dirt that had settled in the lines in her face was gone, as were the matted areas of hair. Her eye was still black and blue, but when you looked at her in profile on the good side of her face, you could see that she would once have been a pretty lady.

Marmie had decided to show me some attention while her new BFF was absent showering, but as soon as Elspeth reappeared Marmie jumped on her lap and began to purr.

'I'm going to whip up some dinner. Do you have any food allergies?'

'Luv, if it's edible I'll eat it.'

After fifteen minutes I'd created a basic spaghetti bolognese. Elspeth carried Marmie over to the dinner table and left her sitting on her lap while she sat to eat. It was clear neither of them was going to let dinner intrude on their bonding.

'So how did you come by this wee darling?' Elspeth asked as she picked at her pasta, handing small morsels to Marmie.

'Someone dumped her in my bin. She's lucky to be alive.'

'I know the feeling,' Elspeth said smiling.

I couldn't quite grasp how she could feel lucky and not consumed with anger.

'I'm determined to find the person who dumped Marmie. In fact, a friend and I are going to visit some people selling kittens tomorrow morning to see if they might be the culprits.'

Elspeth dangled a string of spaghetti in front of Marmie, which was Marmie's two favourite things in the world combined: food and chasing string. I really wanted to ask that she stop feeding Marmie, because I would have to be the one to clean up if human food made her sick. Not to mention, Marmie was flicking tomato sauce everywhere as she pounced on the spaghetti. I went to speak, but Elspeth's laugh stopped me in my tracks. So what if I had to wipe up sauce splatters? Hearing Elspeth happy, in light of the day's events, was priceless.

As I cleared the dishes, Elspeth asked, 'Is it okay if I turn on the TV?'

I turned to Elspeth. 'I want you to feel at home, you know mi casa, es su casa.'

Elspeth screwed up her face, 'Huh?'

'Treat my house as your house.'

A smile spread across her face. 'Thanks luv.'

I tiptoed out of my bedroom, not wanting to wake Elspeth asleep on my couch. I could see the bottle of vodka that had been in my freezer was sitting discarded in the recycling pile. I guess when I told Elspeth to treat my home as hers she had taken it to heart. As long as my alcohol was all that went missing, I didn't mind, although it would make such a difference to her life if she could ditch her addiction.

I waited outside my front door for Sam, not because I wanted to appear super eager to see him, but because I had to check on my bee farm. The weeds were flourishing in my front yard. I patted myself on the back for being such a greenie.

I turned to look up the street for the hundredth time since I came outside and to my delight saw Sam loping towards me. He was so handsome and his smile was contagious. I wasn't sure if his smile was so captivating because his white teeth shone in contrast to his olive skin, or whether it was the way his smile crinkled his eyes, making it seem like you were in on an inside joke.

He wore a simple grey sweater that hugged his broad chest. Memories of being hugged by him yesterday flooded my mind. What I wouldn't give to be enveloped in another of his bear hugs.

'Hey,' I said, feigning nonchalance.

'You ready to catch the cat dumper?'

'You bet. I thought we should get a coffee en route, so we have an excuse to discard our cups in their bin so we can see what bin liners they use.' I didn't think it was necessary to add that then this morning would feel like a cute coffee date.

'Good thinking.'

As I drove towards the address, the plumy sounding voice of the in car GPS navigator kept interrupting our discussion. Why did she need to keep repeating to "stay in the lane and continue on for five hundred meters"? Surely she could just tell me when to not stay in the lane.

I drove towards a roundabout and she interrupted again. "Take the second exit." I had to start counting the number of exits. Couldn't she tell me to go straight through the roundabout? I wanted to mute her annoying instructions, but my car wouldn't allow me to interact with my GPS while driving. Damn that exasperatingly posh English woman constantly talking at me. She had the upper hand, and she knew it!

We drove down a main road with streets splaying off at regular intervals. "Turn left in seven hundred metres". Who knew how far seven hundred metres was? In my head I was thinking it was obviously less than the distance I ran in high school for the eight hundred metres, but more than the two hundred metre race. Why couldn't she just tell me it was the fifth road on the left? I slowed down and as I reached each road, I could see it wasn't that street. Eventually, as I crawled along at walking pace, someone honked me and gave me the bird as they overtook me. I almost missed the turnoff in the commotion. To Sam's credit, he sat quietly in his seat, keeping to himself his dismay at my spatial awareness.

After I parked the car, perfectly I might add, since Sam may have been querying my driving ability, we walked up to the front door of a cookie cutter display home. I rang the doorbell and was greeted by a woman in her fifties.

'Come through. The kittens are in here.'

'Do you have a bin I can put these coffee cups in?'

'Sure, just this way.'

The lady pointed me to a large plastic bin in the corner of the kitchen. I pushed the flap back and peeked into the bin. She used regular black garbage bags. I discarded the cups and turned around. Sam looked at me expectantly and I gave him a discreet shake of my head.

'We have three girl kittens and two boys.'

I looked at the adorable litter of kittens. My fear had been realised – I did want to take them all home. They were a mix of black and grey bundles of fur.

'What colour is the mother cat?'

'She is black.'

'So can she only have black and grey kittens? Would it be possible for her to have a ginger kitten?'

'Hypothetically she could but not this time as she was mated with another black cat. Genetically two blacks can't make a ginger. A ginger cat is only created if both parents carry the red gene.'

I looked across to Sam holding two kittens that were mewing as they rubbed themselves against his chest. He smiled and at that moment I wanted to take a photo to make my screensaver on my computer. He was so damn cute with those sweet kittens.

'They are all so adorable, but I really had my heart set on a ginger cat. Thanks for your time.'

The lady walked us to the front door. 'Well if you have no luck, you or your husband can call me to see if I still have any kittens left for sale.'

I felt warmth flood my face. My husband? I didn't want to make a big deal out of her calling Sam my husband, but I half flushed with pride since she had thought that was the case.

Sam had a cheeky grin on his face. Was he expecting me to correct her, or would that make things even more awkward? Instead I just thanked her and bolted to the car.

'Where to now wifey?' Sam said as he sat in the car.

'Well hubby, I don't have any plans. How about we go get some lunch?'

I started the car and the annoying English lady started repeating, 'You have reached your destination.' I knew we were at our destination, that's why we stopped there you irritating twat. I pulled away from the curb and she then insisted on telling me to 'Do a u-turn when safe to do so.' I hit the cancel button, but the GPS wouldn't respond while I was driving. 'Turn left in fifty metres.' She was persistently trying to take me back to where I had just come from. I had to pull over and put the car in park before I could disable the GPS.

'Go away Patricia,' I said as I turned off the navigation.

'Who's Patricia?'

'That's the name I call the annoying English lady on the GPS. Don't you think she sounds like a Patricia?'

'I think she sounds more like Lady Penelope Longbottom.'

I laughed. 'Actually, now that you mention it, I think you are spot on.'

'Farewell Lady Longbottom, your dulcet tones will be missed,' Sam said laughing.

Sitting at a café by the beach, Sam turned to me. 'How many other litters do you have to see?'

'There are eight more litters. I think I could probably call the remaining people and ask what the parent cats look like. If one of them doesn't have a bit of red in the coat, then they can't be the right litter.'

'Smart thinking, plus you could always get their addresses and we can just sneak around on bin night to check out their rubbish to be sure.'

'You should have been a detective.'

'How was Elspeth when you went to visit her

last night?'

'Oh, I haven't told you. Elspeth checked herself out of hospital. She's actually staying with me until that place becomes available.'

'Do you trust her? You hardly know her.'

'She's pretty harmless. The only thing that might go missing is my alcohol.'

The waitress took our order, and I returned to our conversation.

'You wouldn't believe what she had lived through in her life. Three of her siblings and her mum are dead. Her other two brothers just disappeared, so she is completely alone.'

'It really makes you feel humbled to see what a good life we get to live, doesn't it? After I've volunteered at the soup kitchen, I always go home and think that the biggest issues in my life wouldn't even register as a problem in theirs. It's a good wake up call.'

'That's so true. You know it has made me feel like my time could be better spent offering counseling and psychiatric care for these forgotten people, than interpreting dreams. These displaced people might learn to believe in themselves, if someone showed them they have the faith to believe in them. These people are tough, but at the same time so vulnerable.'

'Are you saying you are going to close your business? You've spent so much time building it. That's a huge thing to consider walking away from.'

'I could probably condense my office days to just two days a week, give up the radio sessions and then focus on counseling. I might even go back to university and do my Masters so I'm a fully fledged Psychologist.'

'There's a lot for you to think about.'

'What about your plans? Have you come to any decisions about moving back to Fiji?'

'My mum is coming to visit in a few weeks so I feel like I will have to make a decision by then.'

'Is she coming to visit with the hopes of helping you pack up to move back?'

Sam laughed. 'No. She's coming to visit me for a few days and to spend some time with her sister for a few days.'

'Oh, does your aunty live here?'

'Yes, she lives about fifteen minutes away from

my place.'

'It's good to know that you're not all alone. I sort of think of you as an orphan, living here by yourself.'

'I go to my aunty's place for dinner every few months so she can check up on me.'

Out of nowhere, Kayleigh appeared with her surfboard wedged under her arm. 'Hi guys.'

'Hi Kayls. You know Sam,' I said, resisting the urge to give her a hug as she looked like a drowned rat.

'Yes, of course. Hi Sam.'

'Back surfing I see,' Sam said. 'Did you do any stretching before you went out this morning? You don't want to strain your back again.'

Kayleigh looked like a naughty schoolgirl caught not handing in her homework.

'Um, well, it was only a quick surf, and I wanted to get out before the wind blows out the waves. I'm sorry,' Kayleigh said grimacing.

Sam laughed. 'You're not in trouble. I just want to make sure you remain fit and strong so you can keep surfing. Maybe do some stretches before you completely cool down.'

'Yes sir.'

'Would you like to join us?' I asked, searching to see if I could spot a spare seat to pull over to the table.

'I'm sorry I can't. I'm just grabbing a coffee and then I've got lots of stretches and stuff I have to do. You guys have fun.'

As Kayleigh went to walk away, she winked at me. I looked across at Sam to see if he had witnessed her but thankfully he was distracted looking out at the surf.

By the time we had eaten our lunch, the predicted wind had hit with force, blowing sand up into the café area. Every exposed part of my body felt like it had been sand blasted. I shielded my eyes as I walked to the car.

'It's like my face is getting an intensive exfoliation,' I yelled out over the howl of the wind.

'I feel like we're in a cyclone,' Sam yelled back.

Once we sat in the car, I looked at my reflection in the rear-view mirror. I resembled Medusa with my windswept hair sticking out in every direction. I tried to flatten the fly away hairs without success.

'Close your eyes,' I said to Sam.

'Why?' he asked closing his eyes as commanded.

'Because I don't want you seeing me look like this.'

He opened his eyes and looked at me. 'You look radiant.'

'I look like a cat caught in a tumble drier.'

Sam laughed. 'You look beautiful. Your hair looks gorgeous when it's windswept.'

I rolled my eyes in embarrassment. 'You obviously have sand in your eyes that's impairing your vision.'

'You don't know how to take a compliment do you?'

I shrugged. Of course, compliments make me feel awkward. Who would want to be the type of person to turn around and say, 'Yep, I'm beautiful.' Come to think of it, I wasn't really accustomed to receiving compliments, so I had no experience of how to react when faced with one. I did the only thing I could think to do in the situation. I changed the subject. 'So do you have plans this afternoon?'

'I was going to go for a run, but with this wind, I think I might give it a miss. What are you up to?'

'I think it is perfect weather to sit at home and watch a movie. You're welcome to join me. Well me, Marmie and Elspeth.'

'Sounds like fun.'

When we got home, I opened the door to find Elspeth sitting quietly on the lounge with Marmie curled up in her lap. When Marmie spotted Sam, she jumped down to investigate.

Elspeth stood and stretched. 'Thank goodness Lady Marmalade is awake. I've been sitting still for hours with her sound asleep in my lap. I've been busting for the loo, but couldna bring myself to wake the wee lassie.'

As Elspeth went to use the bathroom, Sam sat on the lounge playing with Marmie.

'Sam, if you pick a movie on Netflix, I'll cook some popcorn.'

Elspeth returned and sat next to Sam on the two-seater shabby chic (okay, not that chic) lounge. This was awkward, I hadn't taken into consideration that there were three of us, but only two seats.

As I brought the bowl of popcorn across to the lounge, Sam got up and gave me his seat. He instead sat on the floor.

'You don't need to sit on the floor. I'm happy to sit there.'

Sam smiled and wiggled his eyebrows. 'I have an evil plan. I figure if I sit on the floor, you might feel the urge to give my shoulders a massage while you sit on the lounge.'

'Is that right?' I laughed. He might think he would be the winner in this situation, but the thought of rubbing my hands all over his muscular shoulders was enticing.

'Okay. I'm happy to give you a massage, but I have to warn you that I'm not a professional like you.'

'It will be nice to be on the receiving end of a massage for a change.'

I sat down and Sam leaned back between my legs. If only Elspeth hadn't been there, who knows where things may have gone. Instead, I had to be grateful that I got to knead his strong shoulders.

The movie started, and I was so engrossed in rubbing Sam's shoulders that I totally forgot to eat the popcorn. Eventually Sam placed his hand on mine to stop me. 'Thanks,' he whispered. I was crestfallen. I could have spent all afternoon running my hands over his body.

I leaned back and tried to focus on the movie, but having Sam still sitting between my legs was distracting. The movie was some goofy comedy about a group of guys camping in the woods. It reminded me of the dream my client had told me the day before and how Sam had come to my rescue by bringing a teddy bear to maul me. Looking at his thick curly hair, I silently made a deal with the love gods that if they could allow Sam to stay in the country and make him fall in love with me, that I would be forever grateful.

My leg began to tingle with that feeling you get before it turns numb, but there was no way I was moving while Sam was sitting in front of me. If my leg was numb, I was sure Sam must have a numb bum from sitting on the floor.

I leaned forward and whispered in Sam's ear, 'Would you like a pillow? The floor must be a bit hard to sit on.'

He turned around, 'Actually, that would be great, if you don't mind.'

Sam lent forward, and I swung my leg around behind him. As I stood, I realised that my leg had transitioned from being tingly to fully dead. I tried to walk, but it felt like someone had replaced my leg with a prosthetic one that I had no control over. I limped, dragging my leg along the floor. The feeling in my leg began to resurface as shooting pains attacked every nerve ending in my foot.

'Are you okay?' Sam asked, watching me look like someone recovering from a stroke.

'Yep,' I replied, stumbling towards my bedroom to fetch a pillow.

I walked inside my bedroom and stood there shaking my leg to try to get blood to flow back into my uncooperative limb.

'What are you doing?' Sam asked. Unbeknownst to me he had followed me into the bedroom.

'I'm trying to get feeling back in my leg.'

Sam laughed. 'I wondered why you were walking like a pirate with a peg leg.' He bent down and began massaging my calf.

I looked down at him and silently willed him to move his hand higher. I imagined him throwing me on the bed and running his hands all over my body. I could feel my heart rate rising at the thought of it.

'Is that better?'

'Uh huh.' I couldn't trust myself to form an actual sentence. I lent over and picked up a pillow off my bed and then turned around, accidentally smacking Sam in the head with the pillow. 'Oops, I'm sorry, I didn't realise you were still down there.'

Sam grimaced. 'I can't get up. My back is in spasm. Can you help me onto the bed?'

Out of all the number of times I had envisioned having Sam in my bed, never had it been under these circumstances.

I crouched and tried to get his arm around my shoulders and then together we managed to heave his hundred kilo body up and onto the bed.

As he sucked in deep breaths, I tucked the pillow under his head.

'You're a supreme athlete. How did that happen?'

'I used to be a supreme athlete, but now I'm just a guy with a string of left over injuries from my playing days.'

'What can I do for you?'

'Have you got a heat pack and some muscle relaxants?'

I walked back through to the kitchen and noticed that while the movie still droned on in the background Elspeth had nodded off to sleep.

I returned to my bedroom with a warm heat pack and some painkillers.

'Would a massage help?' I asked, more for my pleasure than for his medical requirements.

'A deep tissue massage might help, but not one of your fairy light tickles.'

I pouted. I'd thought my earlier effort had given him a relaxing massage, but instead I'd just been tickling his shoulders.

'You seem like a sensitive guy to me. I didn't want to make you wince in pain by digging my fingers deep into your muscles.'

Sam grinned. 'Don't get me wrong, I enjoyed the massage, but it's not what I need to heal my back. Once these painkillers kick in, I should be able to move okay. Feel free to go back to watching the movie.'

'Nah. I wasn't that into it, plus Elspeth is asleep so I don't want to disturb her.'

I walked around the bed and lay down on the opposite side of the mattress. Lying on my side with one arm propped under my head, I smiled at Sam. 'I bet you didn't expect me to get you into bed today.'

'Definitely not with your chaperone out on the lounge.'

I laughed. It was so easy to be around Sam. I'd never had such fun and playful banter with Jason. He had always been so cerebral and intense.

'Since we have time to kill, tell me why an eligible bachelor like you doesn't have a girlfriend.'

'When I was playing, I was so dedicated to training and travelling with the team that I didn't really have time for a girlfriend. Since retirement, I've dated girls off and on over the years, but they all seemed to be more interested in their Instagram feeds than me as a person. Now your turn, why is a gorgeous girl like you single? Is there an ex-boyfriend in the background, pining about you leaving him with a broken heart?'

I laughed. 'I was in a relationship for about eighteen months. I thought things were okay between us. He thought he'd trade me in for his ex-girlfriend.' I could hear the bitterness seeping into my voice.

'So you're the one with the broken heart?'

'I won't lie. It did hurt when I found out he'd cheated on me and then dumped me. It's almost two years ago now, so I'm truly over him.'

'How did you two meet?'

'He owns the computer store under my work.'

'The one with the random cat poo in the window?'

I laughed. Obviously I wasn't the only one who had noticed. 'Yes.'

'So you still see him all the time?'

'I try to avoid seeing him, but I catch glimpses of him and his girlfriend now and then. I slink around like a loser trying to evade him.'

Sam entwined his fingers in mine. 'I think he is the loser. He needs his head read letting you go.'

I wanted to kiss Sam with every fibre of my being, but I still didn't know where we stood. One moment I thought he was keen on me, the next I wondered if he was just a kind person that says nice things to make people feel better about themselves.

I placed my thumb over his. 'I win the thumb war.'

'That's not fair. You didn't do the countdown to war.'

'One, two, three, four, I declare a thumb war.' I maneuvered my thumb to go over his and then just as I thought I had his thumb trapped, he slid his large, strong thumb over to pin my thumb down under his.

'Ha. I win,' he said. 'I have to warn you, I'm a bit competitive.'

I grinned. 'Me too. Best of three?'

I counted down and again within a few seconds he'd trapped my thumb.

'Okay. Time for me to shine buddy.' I counted down again and managed to trap his thumb for a few seconds. I claimed victory even though technically I may not have held his thumb down for the full three seconds.

Sam wriggled to get in a better position, even if it meant triggering pain across his back. I counted down again, and he had given up any pretext of trying to let me be competitive. My thumb was trapped within a nanosecond.

'I'm the champion,' he said gleefully, raising our linked hands in victory. He then placed a gentle kiss on the back of my hand before placing our hands back on the bed.

Butterflies fluttered in my stomach. Spending time with Sam was like torturously slow foreplay. I just wanted him to make a move that was a definite sign that he was keen on me.

'Do you mind if I have a nap? It might help relax the muscles in my back.'

'That's fine,' I said rising to leave.

'Stay,' he said quietly.

I lay back down beside Sam, our hands still intertwined. There was no way I was going to be able to sleep, but the thought of spending quiet time holding Sam's hand was too irresistible to turn down.

Within a few minutes, Sam's breathing had slowed and turned into deep rhythmic breaths in and out. There was something quite intimate about lying close to someone, watching them in their vulnerable state of sleep. Until that point, I hadn't noticed Sam's long dark eyelashes. At rest, they looked like a perfect set of false lashes. Girls paid good money to get lashes as voluminous as his. They were so wasted on a man. I examined his smooth milk chocolate skin and dark curly hair, imagining how he might have looked as a boy growing up in Fiji.

Sam cracked one eye open, 'I know you're watching me.' I flung my head back onto the pillow, mortified to be caught out examining him. To cover this up, I made some loud, pig like snorts, hoping that if I feigned snoring, he would think I was asleep. He chuckled, squeezed my hand and went back to snoozing.

To my surprise, I actually did fall asleep at some point. It wasn't until Marmie jumped up on the bed and started licking my face with her rough tongue, that I woke. I slowly extricated my fingers from Sam's and tip-toed from the room.

Elspeth was in the kitchen making tea, humming to herself. She grinned when she saw me. 'Oh luv, I can't tell you how lovely it is to be able to make myself a cup of tea. It's the little things in life.'

I smiled. It wouldn't even occur to me to be grateful for a cup of tea, as it was something I took for granted.

'Would you like a cuppa too?'

'No thanks,' I replied, unaccustomed to having someone offer to make me tea in my own home.

'Would your boyfriend like one? I'm sorry, I forgot his name.'

I laughed, 'His name is Sam, and he is not my boyfriend.'

'Oh, I thought the way you two were so cute together, that you must be a couple.'

I contemplated saying, 'I wish,' but instead I giggled. 'No, we're just friends.'

'So do you think he'd like a cuppa?'

'Oh, no, he is sleeping.'

'So this friend of your sleeps in your bed, but he's not your boyfriend?'

'Yep,' I replied, realising how she could be confused.

Thankfully the kettle whistled, cutting off our conversation.

I sat at the kitchen table and busied myself, calling each of the remaining kitten advertisements. I ruled out five people based on their description of the parent cats, although still managed to get their addresses if I needed to do random covert bin searches.

The other two sellers agreed to see me the following day. By the end of the weekend, I might have found the cat dumper. This detective work made me feel a bit like I was playing a game of Cluedo – it was Professor Plum in the kitchen with lilac garbage bags.

Sam materialized from out of nowhere, leaning against the door jamb.

'How are you feeling? Did the sleep help?'

'My back's still a bit stiff, but it definitely feels better. At least I can move now.'

Sam shuffled over to the kitchen table. He seemed to have aged ninety years. It gave me an insight into the old man version of Sam.

'I'm going to head home and have a warm Epsom salt bath to see if that helps.'

'Do you want me to come with you?' I asked. 'I mean, not come have a bath, but help you walk home.'

Sam chuckled. 'Yeah, okay.'

As we walked along the street, I looped Sam's arm around my shoulder, strictly for support and not at all because I wanted to snuggle into his warm, muscular torso.

'I've narrowed the search down to two sellers

and have arranged appointments tomorrow with each of them.'

'I'm sorry, but I don't think I will be able to join you. I've texted my work partner Tom, and he is going to come over in the morning to give me a massage and hopefully realign my spine so I can go to work on Monday.'

'That's fine. I'll let you know how I go.'

'I'm worried that if you find the person responsible that they might be dangerous. Please be careful.'

'I'm not going to do kung-fu on them,' I said laughing. 'Karate is more my style.'

'I'm serious Maggie, promise me you won't confront them. Once you know who it is, you should take your evidence to the RSPCA.'

'Okay. Well thanks for your support today. I've had a nice day.'

'So have I.' Sam bent to kiss my forehead and then opened his front door. 'Bye.'

'Bye,' I squeaked in an abnormally high voice. Apparently my vocal cords don't cooperate when my heart is fluttering.

The following morning I drove, with the assistance of Lady Penelope Longbottom, to the first house that was selling kittens. The yard was a bit overgrown, but rather than judge these people as lazy, I chose to view them as fellow bee warriors.

I rang the doorbell, but wasn't sure if it worked. I tried again and still couldn't hear the familiar ding-dong. I waited a few seconds and then tried again.

I gave up on alerting the residents of my arrival on the doorbell and instead knocked on the door.

I could hear heavy footsteps and then a large woman opened the door.

'Frank,' she yelled at the top of her voice, before turning and leaving me standing on the doorstep.

A few minutes passed until a scruffy man appeared at the door. 'You here about the cats?'

'Yes,' I replied.

He opened the door and walked away. I presumed he wanted me to follow him. Even though I wasn't entirely sure I'd been invited in, I walked behind him until he reached a room that was probably once a verandah that had been enclosed.

'Take your pick.'

I looked at the kittens. They were mottled orange, grey and brown. One in particular looked a bit like a moldy sandwich.

'Did you have any pure ginger coloured kittens?' I asked.

'Darl, I'm not hiding any of 'em from you. What you see is what I've got.'

Not that I expected the cat dumper to tell me they had got rid of a kitten. I couldn't imagine why you would get rid of gorgeous little Marmie and keep these kittens. I inspected each kitten individually to see if they had any similar markings, but I couldn't see any resemblance between these kittens and Marmie.

'Thanks for your time. Choosing a pet is a very serious decision. I'll have to think about it and get back to you.'

'Please yourself,' Frank said. 'You know where the door is.'

I wandered by myself back to the front door. As I was leaving, I noticed Frank's wheely bin on a path beside the house. I hurriedly walked to the bin and wrenched open the lid. The stench was overwhelming, but thankfully there were no purple bin liners to be seen.

My heart rate accelerated. That meant the next house I was going to would either be the culprit, or I'd reached a dead end. Lady Longbottom gave me obtuse directions to get to the other address. This house was only two blocks from my place, so it was feasible they could have used my bin. My hands shook as I gripped the steering wheel. I took a deep breath and then stepped out of the car. There was a small brightly coloured plastic play gym in the front yard. Parked next to it was a matching kid's ride on car toy. Surely if these people had children, they couldn't be so cruel as to dump a cat.

I knocked on the door and a girl with a gummy smile and long brown braids opened the door. Okay if they hadn't taught their kids stranger danger, maybe they were capable of this heinous crime.

'Is Mummy or Daddy here?'

'Mummy,' the little girl yelled. 'There's a lady here.'

'I'm coming,' the woman called out.

As she walked to the door, she swept loose strands of hair from her forehead. As I peered at her through the screen door, I felt she looked familiar.

'Hello, I'm Lucy,' she said extending her hand.

'Hi, I'm Maggie. You look familiar to me.'

Lucy shook her head. 'I don't recognise you.'

'Have you seen me for a dream analysis?' I asked, trying to place the face.

'As a single mum with three kids I don't get a lot of sleep and I definitely don't have spare money to get my dreams interpreted. My dream is to be lying by a pool in the tropics with a cocktail in hand, but unfortunately that isn't reality. Anyway, come and have a look at the kittens. Please excuse the toys everywhere. The kids like the house to look like a bomb site.'

We walked into a room where there were two male ginger kittens and two tortoiseshell females, all vying for a felt toy mouse. I had to do a double take to make sure the mouse wasn't real.

Noting the ginger cats, I found it hard to swallow the lump in my throat. How could this woman be capable of being a mother and a murderer?

I plucked up one of the ginger males.

'You know most ginger cats are male. It has to do with the genetics. I was never any good at biology but it's something related to chromosomes or something.'

'I didn't know that,' I replied. 'You learn something new every day.' This little tidbit made

Lady Marmalade even more special as she was considered rare in the world of ginger cats.

'What breed are these cats?'

'They're tabby cats. See the 'M' marking on their foreheads, that is how you can tell they are tabbies.'

I hadn't noticed beforehand, but low and behold, each kitten had a tiny M shape marking on its head. If I ever had to go to a trivia night on cats, I would blitz it with all the useless information I was learning.

A baby cried in the distance.

'Excuse me for a minute, my little boy has woken from his nap.'

I pulled my phone from my pocket and scrolled through photos to see if I had a close up of Lady Marmalade's forehead. I zoomed in on a photo, but the distinct M these kittens each displayed was missing from Marmie's head. She couldn't be from this litter. I relaxed, relieved that I wasn't going to have to dob this lovely mum into the cops.

When Lucy returned, she had a little brown-eyed, blonde boy on her hip. As soon as I locked eyes on the son, I knew why she was familiar.

'I've worked out where I know you from,' I said laughing.

Lucy's eyebrows rose.

'I was walking down the street the other day when your son dropped his whale toy. I squeezed it and it spurted water all over me.'

Lucy began laughing. 'Yes, of course. Sorry about that. Little Zac loves taking his bath toys everywhere. It was obviously still full of the previous night's bath water.'

'I gathered that,' I said laughing. 'Look I won't take up any more of your time. To be honest, I have a kitten about the same age as these kittens. Someone dumped it in my bin. I'm trying to narrow down who did it, but I know it wasn't part of this litter because she doesn't have the M on her head.'

'I can't believe someone could be that callous. That's really dreadful. I hope you find the person and that they get arrested for animal cruelty.'

'Yes, my thoughts exactly. The problem is that you were the last person on my list. I don't know where to look now.'

'Well if it's any solace, at least that little kitten was found by you and I'm sure you have given it a good home.'

'I'm sorry to have wasted your time.'

'It's fine. If I were in your situation, I would do the same thing. That poor innocent kitten is lucky to have you trying to get justice for it.'

SQUARE ONE

As I arrived home, I surveyed my front yard.
Maybe people did view me a lazy pig, given the
weeds that were multiplying in the front lawn.
Sam's lawn always looked neat, so I decided to
check if he had a lawn mower I could borrow. I
firstly transplanted the dandelions into a terracotta
pot I'd found up the side of the house to ensure I
could still help the bees.

I rang Sam's doorbell, and he opened the door,
looking like he was moving more freely.

'Hi. You look better.'

'Thanks. Tom's a miracle worker. I feel so much
better.' The strong aroma of liniment lotion masked
his usual musky scent. He smelt like the locker
rooms in school. 'Come in.'

I walked into Sam's home. I don't know what I'd
been expecting, but it didn't look like a bachelor
pad. It looked more like a magazine spread for

Modern Interiors. He even had indoor plants in the lounge room. I went and rubbed a leaf between my fingers just to be sure they weren't plastic. How did people keep plants alive? I had an orchid once that I'd stupidly thought was an air plant and didn't require water. Within weeks it shriveled and died, leaving me feeling responsible for its demise. I struggled to live with that on my conscience. After that I swore that I couldn't be accountable for the life of another indoor plant.

'How did you go this morning?' Sam asked as he filled the kettle.

I stuck out my bottom lip. 'I hit a dead end. I'm back at square one.'

'I'm sorry to hear that. We can still do the stealthy bin checks,' Sam said in a hopeful voice.

'You know I think it's time to forget about catching the culprit. At the end of the day, I'm lucky to have a sweet little kitten, and I learned today that female ginger kittens are rare, so I'm doubly lucky. I should be thanking the person for giving me her.'

'Would you like a tea or coffee?'

'A tea thanks,' I replied.

'Milky tea, no sugar, right?'

Either Sam was super observant or had been stalking me. 'Yep. How do you know?'

'That's how you drank it yesterday at the café,' Sam replied. My heart warmed a little, knowing he was making note of the little things.

He placed the tea in front of me at his glass and chrome dining table.

'I'm sorry you didn't find out who was responsible for dumping Lady Marmalade, but I'm sort of glad you didn't because I was really worried about what they might do if they knew who you were.'

'That's sweet of you.' I loved that he felt protective of me.

I took sip of tea. 'I don't suppose you have a lawn mower I could borrow?'

'So you've decided to get rid of your bee sanctuary?'

'I've relocated my bee sanctuary. I think I'd better keep old Nosy Norman, my neighbour, happy and actually mow the lawn.'

'I'd offer to do your lawn if I didn't have this bad back.'

'I'm happy to do it myself. I just don't own a mower.'

I placed the empty mug in Sam's sink. It seemed wrong to mess up the perfectly clean kitchen.

'Come with me. My mower is in the shed out the back.'

I followed Sam in the backyard and was shocked to see a spacious and beautifully maintained tropical oasis.

My jaw dropped open. 'Oh. My. God. This garden is amazing.'

Sam smiled proudly. 'It's like my little taste of the tropics.'

We walked to a shed hidden behind a lush hedge of bamboo. I wanted to come and holiday in this yard.

Sam unlocked the shed door and inside was unlike any shed I'd ever seen. Most sheds are a dusty, spider web strewn space with an avalanche of boxes, tools, odds and sods all jammed into the small area. Sam's shed was meticulous. Every tool had a corresponding shadow drawn on the wall behind. This shed gave me more insight into Sam than spending time with him. I walked in and ran my finger along his workbench. As I suspected, there wasn't even a trace of dust. Sam had either cleaned this area as a way to disguise a murder scene or he was extremely particular about his things, verging on OCD.

I wheeled the shiny lawn mower out into the yard. Did he wash it down after every use? I'd never seen a clean lawn mower before.

'I won't be long,' I said as I wheeled the mower down the garden path and out to the street.

A boy rode past on his bike and turned to do a double take, watching me walk along the footpath pushing a mower. If I'd been pushing a pram, he probably wouldn't have paid the slightest bit of attention.

I parked the mower beside my lawn and then grabbed the pull cord to start it. The cord didn't want to budge. I pulled it with all my might and it slowly came out, barely cranking the motor. I'd seen this done a thousand times as a kid, watching my dad mow our lawns every weekend in summer. I grabbed and pulled the cord again and once more it barely spluttered.

Elspeth opened the front door. 'Get agro girl,' she called out.

I gritted my teeth and yanked on the cord. After

ten attempts, I was sweating like a pig. It would have been quicker to cut the lawn with nail scissors.

Elspeth walked over. 'Move aside.'

Frail little Elspeth thought she could start the mower. What a dear little thing. It was sweet she was willing to try.

Elspeth whipped the cord high into the air and the mower roared to life. What the hell? I made a mental note to include rip-cord training in my exercise regime.

I pushed the mower back and forth over the miniature patch of grass. It had taken fifteen minutes to start the mower and two minutes to do the mowing. I emptied the catcher into my bin and then carried it into my laundry sink to wash it with warm sudsy water. I then took a damp cloth and wiped down the outside of the mower. I had to make sure I returned it in the same condition as I had borrowed it. Once it was again sparkling and clean, I walked it back to Sam's house.

With the mower stored away in its specific place in the shed, I knocked on Sam's door.

'It's open. Come in,' Sam called out. 'I'm in the kitchen. I've made lunch.'

My face was red with the exertion of trying to start the mower and the hair around my face was damp with sweat.

'Did you mow all the neighbours' lawns?' Sam asked laughing at my appearance.

'No. Let's just say I have a newfound respect for landscape gardeners. Who knew starting a mower was such a workout?'

Sam placed two bowls of chicken salad down on the glass-top table, which I quietly noted did not have a fingerprint or crumb on it.

'Thank you,' I said, eating hungrily. 'This is yummy.'

'What are your plans this afternoon?' Sam asked as he ate his lunch.

'I have to go into work. My computer isn't syncing with my phone. Do you know much about IT?'

'I can have a look for you,' Sam said.

I had an inkling that anything Sam tried to do, he did well. I'd never been an over achiever, but I was starting to think I should adopt Sam's attitude.

When we finished lunch, Sam packed the dirty

dishes in the dishwasher and wiped down the table and all the kitchen benches. As he did so, I cast my mind back to my house. I was pretty sure the plates from dinner last night and this morning's breakfast were still piled high in the sink. I added keeping my kitchen tidy to my mental list of things to change in my life.

As we walked towards my office, Jason appeared with a computer stuck under his right arm. I was too close to ignore him and it may have appeared neurotic to run in the opposite direction.

'Hi Maggie,' Jason said. 'Long time no see.'

A thin smile stretched across my lips. 'Hi Jason. This is my friend Sam.'

Sam thrust out his arm to shake hands with Jason. With his right arm holding the computer, Jason held out his left hand, and they did this awkward holding hand thing with their hands pumping up and down. It reminded me of how kids in a playground hold hands as they skip. I had to suppress a giggle.

'How have you been?' Jason asked. 'It's weird that you work upstairs, but I never see you.'

I wasn't going to give him the satisfaction of

knowing that I had been purposely avoiding him for the past few years.

'I guess we are both busy. How is life?' I asked, feeling uncomfortable making small talk.

'Yeah, good.'

'I've noticed a cat in your shop. I thought you had allergies.'

Jason sniffed subconsciously. 'Yeah, I have to take an antihistamine every day. Rosie breeds Bengal kittens. She had to pay $1,000 to breed her female with a local male cat, but it will be worth it. Who knew people would pay $2,500 for a kitten?'

'Wow, that's impressive money,' Sam interjected.

'I never expected to have a cat, let alone seven cats. You should come in and have a look. They are the cutest kittens. They're like miniature cheetah cubs.'

'Thanks, but we're a bit busy,' I said, wondering how else to get out of spending one more minute in Jason's company.

'It will only take a minute. Come on.' Jason walked towards the shop and I mutely followed, mouthing 'sorry' to Sam as we went.

Despite myself, I had to admit the kittens were adorable. They belonged in a movie called 'Honey, I shrunk the cheetahs.' Sam and I crouched by the kittens, giving each of them a quick cuddle.

'Jaassooonnn,' a whiny voice called out from the back of the shop.

I couldn't think of anything worse than coming face to face with Rosemary. 'We really have to go,' I said standing to leave. 'Take care,' I said, pulling Sam by the arm to make a quick exit.

'Bye,' Jason said, before walking towards the voice that had summoned him.

Outside on the sidewalk, Sam turned to me. 'Did you count the number of kittens?' he asked.

I shook my head. I'd been so consumed with their cuteness that I hadn't thought to count them.

'There were five kittens,' Sam said.

I did the mental sums. 'Yeah, that's $12,500 just there,' I replied.

'Yeah, but Jason said there were seven cats. If you take away the mother, that leaves six kittens. There was one kitten missing.'

The gravity of what Sam was inferring hit me

hard. 'Are you suggesting that Jason is the cat dumper?'

Sam shrugged his shoulders. 'Should we check out his rubbish bin?'

We walked to the rear of the complex where the tenants' bins were stored. I located the bin with his shop number and raised the lid. I was sickened to see bags of rubbish, all contained in purple bin liners.

I turned to Sam. 'Oh my god, he is the cat dumper. Why would he do that?'

'Obviously people pay a lot of money for Bengal cats, but if you had one that threw back to being ginger, it wouldn't be worth anything. He probably needed to get rid of it, but didn't want to be found dumping it in his bin so he thought he would use yours.'

Anger pulsed through my veins. 'That bastard.'

I stomped my way back to the front of Jason's shop. As I entered, a chime dinged to alert him that someone had entered the shop. Jason stuck his head out from the back area. 'You're back,' Jason said, a quizzical look on his face.

'Why are there only five kittens Jason,' I asked with a caustic voice.

'Because that's the litter.'

'You said there were seven cats.' I stood with my arms crossed tightly across my chest.

'Yeah. There were seven. There was a runty kitten that died,' Jason replied, looking confused.

'It didn't happen to be a ginger kitten, did it?' I could feel my blood pressure rising with my fury.

Looking baffled Jason replied, 'Yes. How did you know?'

'I found the abandoned ginger kitten in my bin Jason. It didn't die. She is actually healthy and well.'

Jason shook his head. 'What are you talking about? Rosy said she disposed of the kitten because it had died.'

Rosemary had emerged from the back of the shop, watching the exchange with curiosity.

Jason turned to Rosy, Posy What's-her-name. 'Rosy?'

'You're just a jealous ex-girlfriend, trying to create problems. You're so pitiful. You need to get over the fact that Jason chose me over you.' She walked up menacingly towards me, trying to get all up in my grille.

I turned to Jason. 'I'm taking my evidence to the police. You're going to get charged with animal cruelty.'

'Wait Maggie. I really don't know what you're talking about,' Jason pleaded.

'You and your girlfriend can tell your story to the cops.'

Kween Rosy launched at me, trying to grab my hair. Sam stepped in and pulled her away, lifting her in the air like a doll. 'It's time to leave Maggie.'

I walked towards the doors as Sam placed Jason's girlfriend down next to Jason. 'Both of you stay away from Maggie or you'll have me to deal with.' It was the first time I'd ever heard Sam sound the slightest bit intimidating.

Jason held his girlfriend's arm, restraining her from attacking Sam. 'I'm not scared of you,' she screamed at Sam. 'Mark my words - you're gonna be sorry you messed with me.'

I'd never seen such a wild look in someone's eyes. I almost felt sorry for Jason being stuck with such a psycho.

Sam calmly turned his back and walked out of

the shop with me. We quickly entered my office, ensuring we locked the door behind us.

I switched on my computer, keen to get my IT problems resolved swiftly so I could get away from the bad energy pulsing around me.

'She's a firecracker,' Sam said shaking his head. 'I'm a bit worried about you being in this office by yourself during the week, knowing that she is downstairs.'

'I'll be fine,' I replied, not believing a word I said.

'Are you going to report this to the police?'

'Absolutely. They deserve to be punished for animal cruelty.'

'I agree, but the police might think it is just a case of a jilted lover wanting revenge. When you look at the evidence, it relies heavily on them using purple bin liners, but I'm sure there are millions of people that use that brand of bin liners. It's not strong evidence. I feel like if you involve the police, it's not going to change what has happened and it might only serve to increase her anger and aggression towards you. Only this morning you were saying that you were going to let it go. Maybe, for peace of mind, you need to leave it.'

I shook my head. 'But, I need to get justice for Marmie.'

Sam placed his hand on my arm. 'Do you think Marmie is going to know? Your safety is more important.'

I took a deep breath. I knew what he was saying made sense, but it seemed so unjust that they wouldn't pay for their cruel acts.

'Maggie?'

'Okay. I won't go to the police.'

'I think that is for the best.'

My computer dinged to alert me that it was awake. Within a few minutes Sam had managed to re-sync my computer to my phone. Was there nothing this man couldn't do? He was a genius.

TRANSFORMATION

When I arrived home, an aroma of bleach permeated the air. In my absence, Elspeth had thoroughly cleaned the house. I didn't realise that a little elbow grease and some gumption was all that was needed to make my kitchen sink gleam. Nor had I known the grout in my bathroom was actually white. I had assumed the owner had chosen grey grout to go with the grey tiles.

'Wow Elspeth, this place is looking amazing.'

Elspeth smiled coyly. 'Heaven knows I haven't had a place to clean for years, but it is like riding a bicycle. I just went back to my days of being a maid and voila.'

I hugged Elspeth. 'Thank you.'

'It's the least I could do.'

I stepped back and looked at Elspeth. Her hair was clean and the bruise around her eye was beginning to fade. She was almost able to look like a normal citizen. An idea sprung to mind.

I walked into my bedroom, closing the door behind me. I retrieved my phone and called Kayleigh.

'Hi Kayls.'

'Hello lovely. I haven't heard from you for a while. I figured you must be busy with a certain tall, dark and handsome stranger.'

I laughed. 'I have so much to fill you in on.'

'I'm all ears,' Kayleigh replied.

'For starters, I have a temporary flat mate.'

'Who is it?'

'Her name is Elspeth. She is an elderly lady that I met when I volunteered at a soup kitchen.'

'Sorry, what? You volunteered at a soup kitchen?'

'Yes. I did it so I could see Sam. Anyway, this lovely old lady was so sweet that the next morning I decided to find her to give her a small care package. I found her in the park in town with her face swollen and bruised from being assaulted by her ex.'

Kayleigh gasped. 'That's shocking.'

'I took her to hospital but to cut a long story short, she left there and so she is living with me.'

'Don't let her stay too long. She might think she has squatter's rights.'

I laughed. 'Sam has helped to arrange some accommodation for her, but it's not going to be available for another few days. Anyway, I was wondering if you could do her a favour to help her get back on her feet. You know how your uncle owns a nursing home. Is there any way you could ask him if he would be willing to give Elspeth a job in cleaning? Honestly, and I'm not just saying this, she is a phenomenal cleaner. She has just scrubbed my house, and it's cleaner than I've ever seen it. She has previous experience working as a maid in a hotel.'

'I don't mind asking him.'

'Thanks Kayls.'

'So tell me how things are going with Sam. You two looked cosy on your date the other day.'

'Things are good, but I feel like we are in this weird friend zone. I really like him and I'm pretty sure he feels the same, but he is holding back as he doesn't want to hurt me if he decides to move back to Fiji.'

'You need to tell him it is better to have loved and lost than to have never loved at all.'

'That's pretty profound.'

'They're not my words,' Kayleigh laughed. 'I studied Tennyson in high school.'

'Oh.' I laughed. 'So Kayls, what's going on with you?'

'Same old, same old. I don't have anything exciting happening in my life. I have to live vicariously through you. How is Marmie doing?'

'Oh, I forgot to tell you. I've worked out who the cat dumper is. You'll never guess who.'

'Who?'

'Jason and his crazy girlfriend.'

'Wait, what?'

'Yep.'

'Are you going to the police?'

'Sam has convinced me I shouldn't, after Kween Rosemary attacked me. She is one psycho bitch. He is worried she will be out for revenge if I dob them in to the police.'

'I guess it's not worth it if you might end up harmed. Who knows what she could do if she can heartlessly dump a live kitten in a bin.'

'I know. I should just be grateful that I saved Marmie. You know she is selling her kittens for $2,500 each. I'm lucky that I got one for free.'

'Maggie, I'm sorry, there is another call coming through that I need to take. Let's catch up for dinner soon.'

'Okay, bye.'

I walked out into the lounge room to find Elspeth sitting playing with Marmie on the lounge. 'I don't want to get your hopes up, but I've asked a friend of mine to see if her uncle can get you a job as a cleaner in a nursing home. I'll let you know what he says.'

Elspeth smiled coyly. 'I sort of overheard your conversation. Thank you for that. Also for the record, I'm not that old.'

I smiled. 'You are only as old as you feel, right?'

'Maggie, I'm fifty-five. I'm hardly a sweet little

old lady.'

I regarded Elspeth with new eyes. I had thought she was more like seventy-five. The years had certainly been rough on her.

'Oh, I'm sorry. I didn't mean to offend you.'

'Don't be silly.'

'Would you be open to me dying your hair? I think you would look a lot younger without grey hair.'

'Have you done that before?' Elspeth asked.

'When I was a teenager, I did a week's work experience in a hair salon, so I'm practically qualified. I had thought I wanted to be a hairdresser. In that week I realised two things: one – it wasn't the career for me as they stood on their feet all day, and

two – I was more interested in the interaction with clients. Hairdressers are like counselors, so it was that work experience that convinced me I should do a psychology degree, so I could help people with their problems, without having aching feet.'

'I'm game. Let's do it,' Elspeth said.

By the end of the day, I had dyed Elspeth's hair a light brown and had cut her hair. I had initially been planning on just trimming the ends, but I seemed incapable of cutting a straight line. Each time I checked, one side was shorter than the other. Eventually, when her hair was just above her shoulders, I was finally convinced I had managed to make it even. I blow dried her hair and then led her into the bathroom to look at the end result.

Elspeth leaned into the mirror to get a close look at her reflection. Tears welled in her eyes. 'I don't even look like me.' She touched her hair and smiled as the tears burst the dams of her eyes and streamed down her face.

I'm such a sook. At the first sign of tears, I started to cry too. A simple change to Elspeth's hair had erased years off how old she looked.

'I look like I did twenty years ago. Thank you.'

'I can't believe the transformation. Maybe I should have been a hairdresser.'

'I didn't think I wanted a bob, but my hair feels so light and it looks so glossy. I feel like I am on one of those reality make over shows.'

'You look great. There's just one thing. Turn around.' I retrieved my makeup bag and located a foundation I'd bought a few years ago that was too light for my skin tone. I smeared some on a sponge and wiped it gently over Elspeth's face, concealing the remnants of her black eye. I then slicked on a rose coloured lipstick.

When I turned her around to look at her reflection once more, her face glowed with pride.

'You are a miracle worker. Look at me.'

'You look beautiful. Imagine that you go to job interviews looking like this. There won't be any judgement on the way you present yourself.'

Elspeth wrapped me in her arms. 'Thank you luv. My guardian angel was looking out for me the day I met you.'

DREAM TIME

I arrived at work early to ensure I wouldn't encounter the wrath of Jason's girlfriend on my way to the office. After entering, I locked the door behind me to be safe.

Once I had completed some bookwork, a soft knock on the door alerted me that my first client had arrived.

'Come in Lauren,' I said, ushering the shy young lady to the seat.

'Thank you.'

'What inspired you to come see me?'

'I'm fascinated by dreams. I'm doing a project on dreams and people's subconscious. One day I'd love to have a job like yours.'

I refrained from telling her the hazards of the job.

'Do you have a dream in particular you would

like analysed? I'll just ask that you don't share with me dreams about death and destruction. I get so drawn in to some people's dreams that I find those dreams can leave me feeling triggered.'

She nodded. 'Umm, it's a bit embarrassing, but I have a recurring dream of me standing in public in my underwear and everyone is staring and laughing at me.'

I instantly had a sinking feeling in my gut. This was up there with my greatest fears and I was immediately running through scenarios in which this might play out for me, none of which was okay.

'I try to put a robe on, but it keeps getting pulled away just out of reach. I'm so mortified that I just stand there like a dummy.'

My stomach was curdling with the thought.

'How do you feel after waking from this dream?'

'I'm embarrassed and humiliated. That feeling seems to stay with me all day, even though logically I know it is just a dream.'

'Dreams of being seen in public naked or in underwear are the brain's way of telling us that you feel inadequate. Do you feel excluded at school?'

'Sort of. I'm not in the cool group. I mean I do

have friends but I've never had that one BFF, like you see in all the Disney channel sitcoms.'

'Does that make you feel like there is something wrong with you, if you don't have a best friend?'

'It does a bit, but like I said I have a group of friends, so it's not like I'm socially isolated.'

'Do you have a boyfriend, or a boy you like?'

Lauren's face blushed bright red as she shook her head. 'I don't have a boyfriend.'

'Someone you like?'

I didn't know it was physically possible for her face to deepen in colour, but not only did the colour of her blush deepen, but it spread down her neck. 'Umm.' She giggled. 'Sort of.'

'I don't want to get too personal, but if you are open to talking with me, you can know this is confidential.'

'There is a guy called Jack. We are friends, but I'm not sure he realises I like him.'

I nodded. I knew this scenario all too well.

'Have you considered telling him that you like him?'

'Shouldn't the guy chase the girl?'

'Not necessarily. How will he know that you are keen if you don't tell him? Are you worried that you won't measure up?'

'He is really cute. I'm not sure that he would be interested in me. What if I tell him and he rejects me and then things get awkward? Isn't it better to have his friendship than nothing?'

I'd been asking myself this same question for weeks.

'You can't control what the heart wants. Imagine he finds out that you are keen on him, and he is relieved as he didn't want to make a move on you because he wasn't sure if you would reject him.'

'Yeah, but I can't just walk up to him and ask, "Hey, do you want to go on a date?" Could I?'

'Confidence can be a very attractive attribute. If you believe in yourself and know that you are worthy of him and his affection, then maybe he will return the feeling. If not, then you can get closure on your feelings and move on to another boy. Don't you think that would be better than pining silently for someone?'

'When you put it like that, I guess so. It's just that I'm too shy.'

'Can I make a recommendation? Each morning you should start your day with affirmations, like "I am worthy," "I am smart," "I am beautiful." There is research that shows affirmations reset your brain and trick your psyche into believing the things you tell yourself.'

'I knew when I read your article in *Teen Girl* that you would know what my dream was telling me. I didn't know that the analysis would come with helpful guidance. Thank you so much.'

After Lauren left, I reached for my phone. There was a text from Sam. *I've been worried about you. Has everything been ok at your office this morning?*

I replied. *Yes and no. I haven't seen Jason or his girlfriend, but I'm worried about how I'm going to deal with my last client's dream recreation.*

What was the dream?

She was in public, wearing nothing but her underwear. I added an eyes wide, looking shocked emoji.

I received a crying from laughter emoji in return.

I wasn't going to be crying with laughter, rather with humiliation at this turn of events.

My phone tinkled with the magical wind chime ringtone again. *I'd like to be there to see that one.*

I had been hoping Sam was going to be helpful in solving how to deal with this terrifying situation.

I need a solution to hijack this dream that doesn't involve me standing in the middle of town in my underwear. Help me out.

I'm serious.

Sam?

I received a return text. *I'm thinking.*

A few minutes later my phone tinkled again. *I've got an idea. I'll come get you on my lunch break.*

I felt sick with anticipation. Any form of public nudity was way outside of my comfort zone. Maybe he was going to drive me home to his place and seduce me at lunchtime so he would see me in my lingerie. I pulled the neck of my shirt open to peer down at my bra. I was wearing an old cotton bra that was once white but now was a sickly pale grey from being washed with non colourfast clothes. I then tried to recall what underpants I was wearing. I cast my mind back to getting dressed this morning and groaned when I recalled I was wearing a pair of pants with gigantic red hearts all over them. I added to my mental list, buy new lingerie.

At ten past twelve, Sam knocked on my office door. When I opened it he passed me a plastic bag. 'Here, quickly go put these on.'

I peeked in the bag and saw my bikini in the bag. How on earth had he got my bikini?

I raced to the bathroom, changing out of my daggy underwear.

When I returned, I realised that Sam was sporting

boardshorts and a t-shirt, not his usual business attire.

'We don't have long. Come on, we are going to the beach. You can lie in the sun in your bikini and that should hopefully work as the interpretation of being seen in public in your underwear.'

I cringed. This was only a minor step above being seen in my underwear. To make it worse, it was in front of Sam and I wasn't even sure when the last time was that I shaved my legs.

We hurried to Sam's car. As we drove, I turned to Sam. 'How did you get my bikini? Are you some sort of sicko with an underwear fetish? While I slept the other day were you actually rifling through my drawers?'

Sam burst into hysterical laughter.

'I dropped by your place and Elspeth went and found them for me. I hope that is okay.'

Relief flooded through me. I'd been envisioning Sam seeing my messy drawers and him doing a quick Marie Kondo inspired tidy up.

Whilst it was a sunny day, it wasn't particularly warm. I would usually wait until January to go to the beach.

When we got out of the car, I found my feet unwilling to move. My anxiety levels were rising at the humiliation of the imminent unveiling of my body.

Sam walked around and took hold of my hand, tugging me towards the beach, much like a parent dragging their uncooperative child to bed.

'It's not that bad. Come on. I'll strip down too, okay?'

My brain switched out of nervous melt down mode to suddenly feeling a lot more inclined to follow through with this plan.

I reflected back on my advice to Lauren earlier in the day. I silently began chanting mantras. 'You can do this,' 'You are beautiful,' 'You are bold,' 'You are going to see Sam half naked.' Oops, that last one slipped in accidentally.

Sam laid two beach towels out on the sand and then whipped off his shirt. I knew he had a broad chest with well-defined pecs, as I could make that out through his clothes, but I hadn't been expecting the rock hard six-pack. This day wasn't actually turning out to be as bad as I'd thought.

'Your turn,' Sam said smiling.

I took a deep breath, and quickly removed my

clothes and threw myself down on the sand, burying my face in the towel.

'See it wasn't that hard was it?' Sam said, smiling. It was lovely he was so confident in his skin, but not all of us looked like Greek gods, or should I say Fijian chiefs?

Sam brushed some sand from my back and my skin tingled where his fingers touched my flesh.

'I'll give you ten minutes to stop that,' I said, practically purring at his touch.

'Ha ha. There are worse ways to spend a lunchtime,' he said dragging his fingers lightly over my back. I felt like I was going to implode with delight.

'Are you keen to swim?' Sam asked.

I screwed up my face.

'I'll take that as a no then?'

'That's a hell no!' Little did he know that the bikini he had packed for me barely contained my ample bosom. There was no way I was going to risk a nip slip in the surf.

'It seems wrong to not swim when I'm at the beach. I'm just going to have a quick dip.'

As Sam walked towards the surf, I rolled onto my back to maximize perve potential.

He was enjoying himself body surfing in the waves. There was nothing he couldn't do. I was worried that maybe I was suffering from psychosis and I was hallucinating that Sam was the perfect man. Surely the man had faults. I wouldn't rest until I'd discovered his imperfections.

I quickly wrapped my towel around my waist to form a sarong like skirt. As Sam neared, I could see that he was struggling to keep his eyes on my face. I nervously tugged at the sides of my bikini top, wishing it had better coverage.

Sam's hair held little droplets of water that sparkled in the sunshine. As he got closer he shook his hair, showering me in salt water.

'You didn't want to go in the ocean, so I brought a little of the ocean to you.'

'Gee thanks,' I said sarcastically.

'I can see why you didn't want to be seen in public in your underwear.' I tugged at my bikini top again, wishing that it gave me a little more dignity. 'That is way too much sexiness to display in a public area.'

I rolled my eyes.

'I'm surprised you haven't been mauled by every passing man.'

I self-consciously put my dress shirt back on.

'I guess we had better get back to work. Thanks for coming to my rescue once again.'

'I enjoyed this. Maybe we should make it a regular thing, like some offices have mufti Friday, we could have beach day Mondays.'

Sitting in the car on the way back to the office, Sam casually mentioned his mum was going to be in town Friday week and asked if I would like to join them for dinner. I had a quick look at my calendar; I had the photo shoot for Levi in the morning and a session mid-afternoon on that Friday with a woman with an Indian sounding name. I had to remember to review if certain dreams are altered by ethnicity. If she came to me with a dream about cows, that may mean she is holy, not just that she is happy. 'I'm free that night. What time should I come to your house?' I asked.

'Just come over after work.'

'Does this mean that you are going to make a decision soon about whether you are going to stay or leave?'

I didn't want to pressure him, but I kept

replaying the advice I had given Lauren earlier in the day about being transparent about your feelings.

'I want to talk it over with my mum and then I'll make my final decision.'

Sam parked the car. I took a deep breath and then turned to him. 'At the risk of making a fool of myself, I have to put this out there. I know it would mean a lot to your mum for you to move back to Fiji, but it would mean a lot to me if you stayed. I really like you and I'd like to see how things could develop between us. I don't want to make you choose, but I also couldn't live with myself if I didn't put up a fight.'

Sam smiled gently, not giving anything away. 'Thanks for sharing that with me.'

I'd hoped for a jump in the air and a click of his heels, or for him to declare his undying love, but having next to no response was even worse than a definite thanks but no thanks.

Feeling embarrassed, I patted his hand and hopped out of the car. 'Thanks for today. I'll see you next week.'

I sat at my desk, feeling the grit of some sand chafing on my all too small bikini top. I didn't have time to change before my next appointment. The door was ajar and when I looked up I was shocked to see Kween Rosy the Psycho Cat Dumper standing in the doorway wielding a box-cutter knife.

'You've ruined my life. Jason just dumped me and has kicked me out because of you. He has given me an ultimatum to either confess to the RSPCA or he will call them. Your business might be called Day Dream, but now is your nightmare.'

She lunged at me, knocking my penholder over, spraying its contents across the floor.

I skirted around the desk to try to put more space between us.

'I don't understand. Why would you dump an innocent kitten?'

'No one likes ginger cats. The only ginger cat anyone ever liked was Garfield because he ate lasagna and was a smart arse.'

'That's not true. I love Marmalade. You should have given her free to a good home instead of leaving her to die in my bin. By the way, why did you choose to dump her in my bin?'

'You left me your old Valentine's Day card at Jason's house, thinking that it would hurt me and I'll admit, it did a little. But no-one gets away with hurting me, so I thought I'd give you a little present. That stupid cat should have died and made your bin stink, but you saved it. Now you're making my life hell.'

I racked my brain thinking of how a psychologist would diffuse a situation like this. I think I'd missed the lecture on talking down psychos.

Kween Rosy lunged again, this time hurtling my in-tray across the room to smash into the wall. My neatly written notes were strewn across the floor. My hands shook with fear.

She lunged with the knife once more, nicking the sleeve of my blouse. I screamed with terror. Even though I was almost twice her size, she was dangerous as she slashed her weapon around.

She pounced towards me and her knife sliced through the dream catcher and lodged in the wall. She growled as she pulled the knife out of the plaster and then grabbed the dream catcher by the feathers hanging below and lassoed it, flinging it across the room. It crashed into the opposite wall, the force so strong it splintered the wood in the outside ring.

I edged further around the desk until I had a free path towards the door. I ran up the stairs, screaming for help as I went.

Levi came out of his office to see what the commotion was.

'She's going to kill me. Please help.'

The Kween had raced up after me, but stopped in her tracks when she saw Levi. Within an instant the aggression dropped from her face and she transformed into a sultry seductress. 'Well hello good looking. Where have you been hiding? I'm Rosy, do you want to go out for a drink some time?'

Levi played along. 'Hi, I'm Levi. It's nice to meet you.' His acting had improved remarkably since his first night at acting class.

Levi reached out his hand to shake hers. When she extended her hand, he grabbed it and, overpowering her, he wrapped it up her back. She slashed at his arm with the knife. She was so distracted with the altercation, she didn't notice when I grabbed her arm, squeezing the life out of it until she dropped the knife.

'I have some cable ties in my second drawer. Bring them here and we can restrain her while we wait for the police to arrive.'

I grabbed the cable ties and, while Levi held her hands together against her will, I looped one around her wrists, ensuring it was tight, maybe even a tad too tight, but you could never be certain. I then cable tied her ankles together to ensure she couldn't run away.

I called emergency services, requesting police and an ambulance.

Once that was done I looked to Levi. He was sweating profusely and his face was pale. He was holding his arm where he had been sliced, but the blood continued to ooze out. I grabbed another cable tie and used it as a tourniquet to stem the blood flow.

On the floor, What's-her-name writhed, spat and screamed at the injustice. I grabbed her by her feet and dragged her into the supply closet and then closed the door.

'Hello,' a voice echoed up the stairwell.

'We're up here,' I yelled.

A lady in her thirties appeared, wearing a navy jumper over navy pants.

'Are you police or paramedics?' I asked.

'Uh, um, I just here for an appointment at Day Dream Incorporated. Do you know where the woman is who runs it? I think her name is Maggie.'

'Sorry. I'm Maggie. We've had an incident and we are waiting for the police to arrive. I'm sorry to inconvenience you, but can we re-schedule? Maybe tomorrow morning?'

Once Jess, my next client, saw the blood on the floor, she started creeping backwards. 'You know. It's fine. You get this sorted and let me know when it would be best to reschedule.'

She had almost disappeared down the stairwell when I called out. 'Thanks for your understanding. I'll be in contact.'

I could hear sirens nearing until eventually they were deafeningly loud and the alternate red and blue lights were flashing through the open window.

The paramedics arrived first and after a brief evaluation they helped Levi on to a stretcher. I held Levi's hand as I leant over to whisper in his ear. 'Thank you so much for helping me today. Without you I might be dead now.'

'You can't die. I'm relying on you for the shoot on next Friday. Send me flowers and make sure the press hears about this, so that I sound like an amazing hero, okay?'

'You bet,' I said, smiling as they carried him off

on a stretcher.

Moments later police raced up, wearing bullet proof jackets and with their hands on their holsters.

One officer pulled me aside to take my statement, while the other one opened the supply closet door to check on Rosy Posy Bitchface. It's a pity the impenetrable vest didn't cover his genitals, as she kicked him as hard as she could. He crumpled as he slammed the door shut again.

Writhing in pain on the floor, he gasped, 'Moroney, this one is yours.'

The police officer interviewing me wore a confused expression, a mixture between humour and concern. 'Okay Boss,' he replied before returning to taking notes.

By the time I'd finished with the police, Levi had texted that he was getting six stitches and was being sent home with a doctor's certificate stating he didn't have to work for a week. He'd already arranged his director friend to take him on a getaway to far north Queensland to rest and recuperate.

Eventually, the police managed to drag Jason's ex out of the building, with her kicking and screaming the whole way.

As I walked back into my office I was devastated to see the carnage that had been left in the wake of cyclone angry bitch. My confidential notes were strewn everywhere and my beautiful authentic dream catcher was destroyed beyond recognition.

I tidied up and took the rest of the debris down to the bin.

Jason intercepted me at the communal bin area.

'Maggie. Mags. I'm so sorry about all this. I knew Rosy was passionate, but I never expected she could be capable of all the things she has done recently. You know that I thought I needed more excitement in my life, but I should have been happy to settle for you.'

'Gee thanks,' I replied sarcastically. 'Jason, if you weren't happy with me, you should have just left. No one should have to settle in life. You broke my heart cheating on me and then moving your new girlfriend in as soon as you got rid of me. I felt like a piece of trash, but I guess now you know she is the piece of trash.'

Jason reached out and placed his hand on my arm. 'Mags, it's not too late to go back to what we had.'

I looked into Jason's pale blue eyes to check for irony. 'Jason, it is absolutely too late to ever go back there. You left me feeling abandoned and alone, leaving me for your gold digger ex-girlfriend.'

'She told me that she had always loved me and that if she couldn't be with me, then she would kill herself. I thought that was a sign that she loved me unconditionally.'

'You didn't think it sounded like she was mentally unstable? Just so you know, she moves on fast. She asked Levi on a date before she stabbed him.'

Jason looked shocked at this revelation.

I shook his hand from my arm. 'You know karma is a bitch and now you are the one all alone, having to deal with the fall out after bringing this girl here. I don't think you get the gravity of the situation – she almost killed me today. You know she goes under five aliases on social media? Do you even know who she really is?'

With shoulders slumped, Jason slunk away.

After getting home I just wanted to collapse in bed with Marmie. I thought my anger at Jason for bringing his girlfriend back from Queensland had all been used up, but I found I had a renewed fury that he had jeopardized my safety by having her here. I opened my phone and saw that Sam had sent me a text.

How was your day?

I wasn't sure how to respond. I began to type: *I almost died,* but then deleted that, as I didn't want to be too melodramatic. I typed a new sentence: *The cat dumper almost stabbed me,* but then I deleted that. Even a cat emoji with love heart eyes wouldn't soften that statement. I simply typed: *It was a bit of a rough day. I will fill you in when I see you on next.*

Sam responded immediately. My phone alerted me with its angel wing wind chime ringtone.

I'm sorry to hear you had a bad day xx. He added a sad face emoji and just knowing he was there for me, without knowing the drama that had occurred, was enough to calm me.

Rather than sit and stew over the day, I decided to distract myself by opening Facebook to scroll through my friend's posts.

Under the banner of a local news site I saw a photo of Rosy Posy What's-her-name in handcuffs, with the headline, 'Female arrested for assault of local model.' It didn't take long for news to spread. I quickly clicked on the story.

"Rosemary Turner, 38, of Nerang, Queensland, has been arrested over the assault of local model Levi Glaston. Turner had an altercation with Maggie McIntyre of Day Dream Inc, whose business is located under the office of Glaston. Turner confronted McIntyre with a knife after she proclaimed Turner was responsible for dumping a day old kitten in McIntyre's bin.

Davey Winston, from the Davey and Charlie Breakfast show on Fly FM, relayed the story of how McIntyre had found a day old kitten in her bin a few weeks ago and had brought the kitten into the radio station for her regular dream analysis segment. Winston professed how cute the kitten was and how shocked not only he, but his listeners and fellow workmates had been, to hear that someone had dumped the poor innocent kitten.

Turner is known to police and has been issued with a warrant for her extradition to Queensland. She fled Queensland nine months ago when she was on parole for previous crimes that include assault occasioning actual bodily harm, attempted homicide, disturbing the peace, possession of concealed weapons and driving whilst unlicenced.

Celebrity model Glaston received stitches as treatment for the stab wound and has now been released from hospital."

The article was then interrupted by an advertisement for kitty litter – I swear my social media was listening to my conversations about Marmie, because I suddenly had my feed swamped with cat related ads. I vowed to start talking more about sexy men with six packs wearing only underpants to see if that would impact the advertising I received. When I finally scrolled past the kitty litter ad, the article just discussed Levi's advertising campaigns and his rise to fame as a social media influencer. I was sure Levi would be happy with the article, as he loved any publicity. Clearly Davey also loved publicity, as it was odd that he had made a comment for the article. His opinion of Marmie seemed to have changed since he met her, but I guess he thought it was best to be seen to be sympathetic for the cat.

I couldn't believe Rosemary was a fugitive on the run. Then again, after I'd seen her psycho behaviour, it wasn't that hard to believe. The parole in Queensland must have been the trouble she had found herself in, that was the reason for her contacting Jason to be her knight in shining armour.

I wondered if Jason had known he was harbouring a criminal?

I turned off my phone. There was no escaping the psycho who was trying to ruin my life. At least she wouldn't be able to attack me again now that she was being sent back to Queensland, hopefully to spend time in a prison cell.

AWAKENED

I re-scheduled Jess for the following morning, although I could tell she was hesitant to come after the vicious attack that had occurred at my premises the day before.

I could tell from our phone conversation that Jess was feeling jittery, so I had brewed a cup of chamomile tea to help calm her nerves.

I ensured she saw me lock the door behind her, which apart from appeasing her, also soothed my nerves.

'Jess, I'm so sorry about yesterday. It was a crazy day.'

'Was she one of your clients who didn't agree with your analysis?'

I laughed. 'No, she was the crazy girlfriend of my ex-boyfriend. She was out for revenge.'

'How scary for you.'

I nodded. It had kept me awake all night, running through scenarios of 'what if.' I was feeling lucky to be alive, and it gave me renewed enthusiasm to help victims of domestic violence. I'd even lodged an online application with my university to complete my Masters in Psychology while I was wide awake at 3am.

'So Jess, tell me about your dream.'

'I had this dream a few weeks ago that was so realistic. I was on stage singing and I was so filled with joy. A scout for a recording company was there and asked me if I would be interested in being signed by him. You see, I do musical theatre as a hobby. I was so excited when I woke, that I wondered if this is a sign that I might be on the verge of being discovered?'

Jess was on the rounder side of chubby and already in her thirties. I didn't have the heart to tell her it was likely that boat had already sailed.

'Remember the joy you felt when you awoke? The reason for that is because dreams of singing on stage are symbolic of peace and happiness. You may not be about to be the next Beyonce, but I'm guessing you are in a pretty happy place in your life.'

Jess nodded. 'I guess so. I'm happily married with two daughters. We own our own home and go on holidays each year. Come to think of it, you could definitely say I'm happy.'

'It is very easy to take the good things in life for granted. It is important to take a moment to reflect on the things for which you are grateful. There are studies that show people who keep daily gratitude diaries experience a higher level of joy. Your brain is just trying to make you aware how happy you are and as you enjoy musical theatre, it has come to you in your dream state as singing on a stage.'

While I was talking, I was considering how this dream was going to play out. I am totally tone-deaf when I sing. Kayleigh on the other hand is an amazing singer. Maybe we could go to karaoke bar and we could sing together. Maybe her singing would drown out mine, or maybe a talent scout would be looking for someone with no musicality and a voice to match.

Jess nodded. 'You are right. I am so lucky. It's time I was grateful for everything in my life. I don't need a recording contract to bring me happiness, my life brings me happiness.'

After my session, I reviewed my phone

notifications. I'd missed a call from Sam. I retrieved the voicemail to hear his excited voice. 'Hey Maggie, that charity called, and a room is now available for Elspeth. If she can pack her things, I can duck over on my lunch break to help her move.'

I was speechless. I was a big believer that if you put something out to the universe, it would listen and provide.

I called my home phone. I'd tossed up getting rid of it since I'd moved in as I'm always an arm's distance to my mobile phone, but my parents insisted that everyone needs a landline.

Elspeth answered hesitantly, 'Maggie's residence.' It sounded like I had called some quaint little bed-and-breakfast.

'Hi Elspeth, it's me, Maggie. I have great news. Sam just heard that the room has become available for you. He said if you pack your stuff, he will move you over on his lunch break.'

A sob escaped Elspeth. 'Thank you. You are all wee angels sent to guide me.'

I wasn't sure if she had been sipping on the wine in the fridge, or whether she meant we were figurative angels. Either way, her gratitude was clear.

No sooner had I hung up from Elspeth than I received a text from Kayleigh. *My Uncle John said Elspeth can do a trial week at the nursing home, starting Monday. He will decide after the week if she can have a job. They pay award wage and it's a hard slog.*

If Elspeth thought her prayers had been answered, she would be over the moon with this news.

I called the home phone again. Elspeth answered once more, 'Maggie's residence.'

'Elspeth, I've just heard that you can do a week's trial at that nursing home.'

'Is there a camera hiding somewhere? This is too unbelievable. Are you kidding me?'

'No, it's real. The pay is only award and after a week, they will decide if your quality is good enough to offer you a full-time job.'

'Thank you so much.'

'You deserve it. You know I'd do anything to see you happy, healthy and well.'

'Can I have Marmie?' Elspeth asked hopefully.

'Nice try. No I'm sorry, she's my cat, but once you are settled, you could ask if they are open to you having a pet.'

'You know I keep thinking back to a week ago. I was homeless, fearful and with no prospects. I'm now going to have a home, a job and true friends. None of this would have been possible without you. I truly owe you my life.'

'You don't owe me anything, except maybe a bottle or two of wine.' The last time I'd taken the recycling out to the bin I was shocked to see multiple empty wine bottles. At no time had Elspeth appeared drunk, but she very clearly had a drinking problem. I wanted to address this with her, but for the moment it was baby steps. As long as she could do a job and maintain her room that would be a huge leap forward for her.

I texted Kayleigh back. *Hello lovely. That is amazing news. Elspeth is thrilled. Any chance you'd like to have dinner, drinks and a karaoke tonight?*

My phone buzzed immediately. *You had me at hello.*

7pm tonight at Riley's?

It's a date.

I ducked home after work and the place seemed so quiet and empty without Elspeth on the lounge. Marmie was extra attentive to me since her favourite human had disappeared. Cats are so fickle.

I threw on a sparkly top and a pair of jeans. I may not sing like a rock star, but at least I could look like one.

At 7pm, I walked in to the bar. Kayleigh was already at a table busily filling out entry forms. By the time I returned to the table with drinks she had submitted them without my review.

'What are we singing?'

'You'll see.'

I bet she had put down all Mariah Carey songs in a range that only dogs can hear. I would have requested a Bob Dillon song because that way you could speak the lyrics.

We quickly ate some fried chicken wings and wedges, as I slurped on my wine for Dutch courage.

'It's not like you to suggest karaoke,' Kayleigh said.

'It was one of my client's dreams. I thought this would get the dream out of the way.'

The lights dimmed, and a spotlight beamed down on the MC. 'Thanks for coming here ladies and gentlemen, and those not so gentle men at the back.' He laughed at his corny joke.

'The first act up tonight is the Pointy Sisters, with "I'm so excited." Give them a hand.'

Kayleigh nudged me. I turned and looked at her. 'Please tell me you didn't call us the Pointy Sisters.'

Kayleigh held her hands up to her bust with her fingers pointing out, looking like some weird fembot. 'Of course I did. Now come and be excited.'

I seriously didn't have enough alcohol coursing through my veins to have an ounce of desire to get up to sing, but if suffering from dream transference had taught me anything, it was to embrace being out of my comfort zone.

Kayleigh grabbed my hand and dragged me towards the karaoke machine.

The lights were blinding on stage. On a positive note, I couldn't see anyone in the audience. The negative was that I wasn't sure I would ever be able to see again without big black spots blocking my vision.

Kayleigh sang with vigor. She did truly seem excited. I sang quietly in the background and followed her semi-choreographed moves, trying to pull off the girl band vibe. When we finished, I was shocked to hear loud clapping and whistling. Maybe I had missed my calling in life.

Over the course of the night we got up five times to sing. Each song I sang louder and with more enthusiasm (and coincidentally, more alcohol in my system).

Our final cover of the night was Bohemian Rhapsody. I nailed the operatic part, if I say so myself. The whole pub was up singing and so by the time I was ready to go home I had a feeling of inner happiness and peace, similar to the way Jess' dream left her feeling. My feeling might have also been due to a bottle of wine and a margarita, but really, who is to say?

SLEEP IN

I rushed towards my office when I saw a dark-haired lady loitering outside the door. I was running late as Marmie decided to hack up a furball onto my freshly pressed linen blouse. I then had to try to find another blouse to wear. Having fallen a bit behind with my washing, I extracted the cleanest looking blouse out of my dirty wash basket. I sniffed the armpits, which weren't too offensive. I then quickly ironed it and sprayed a mist of perfume all over it to hide the fact that it wasn't totally fresh.

I was flustered and couldn't remember the name of my first client for the day.

'Sorry I'm late,' I said thrusting my hand at her. 'I'm Maggie.'

'I'm Kerry,' she said shaking my hand enthusiastically. 'Did you sleep in?' she asked smiling.

'I wish. Unfortunately I had a wardrobe

malfunction thanks to my cat.' I jangled the keys, trying to fit the key in the lock. The more I rushed, the more the key refused to fit. 'The lock is a bit temperamental,' I said before I accidentally dropped my keys. What a way to look professional!

'I used to live in an old cottage around here when I was first married. You had to wiggle the key and hold the door handle on a certain angle and then it might cooperate and open.'

While Kerry had been talking, I'd managed to take a deep breath, retrieve my keys and unlock the door.

'Come inside. Please take a seat.'

A shiver ran down my spine as I saw a crack in the plaster behind my desk, where what's-her-name psycho wench had smashed the dream catcher that had once decorated my office. I opened a window to let in fresh air, started my computer and put on the kettle.

'Would you like a cup of tea or coffee? I think I could do with some caffeine this morning.'

'A black coffee would be great.'

While the kettle boiled, Kerry told me about her husband, kids and job. One thing I loved about my job was meeting so many different people and getting insights into how they lived.

I finally sat at the desk with a coffee in hand. 'Okay Kerry, tell me all about your dream.'

'Well I had a dream the other night, and it was on the anniversary of my mother's death. I was in a field of flowers and there were colourful blooms as far as the eye could see. There was a light misty rain, but it wasn't making me wet, it was only nourishing the flowers. I could see my mother in the distance and she was spinning around in circles with her arms outstretched. My mum always loved gardening and her flowerbeds were her pride and joy. When I woke, I had the distinct feeling that I had actually visited my mum in heaven.'

'That is really lovely Kerry.'

'Do you think it is possible to connect in your dreams with loved ones that have passed over?'

'I don't really know about that. There are definitely people who believe you do and then there are just as many skeptics. I can't say either way for sure, but what I can tell you is what a field of flowers symbolizes. It is a very fortunate thing to dream of flowers as they reflect happiness and spirituality. The fact that you saw your mum in the field of flowers and she was outwardly showing her joy reinforces this interpretation. Your mum must have been on your mind as it was the anniversary of her death, which is a possible reason that she was in the dream. Our love for people doesn't disappear when they die, so it must have felt very comforting for you to dream of seeing your mum again and for her to be surrounded by a field of flowers.'

After the morning I'd had, I'd half expected the dream to be about snakes, sharks or poison darts. I was relieved Kerry had dreamed of flowers, as I would be happy to be given a random bouquet.

'I woke that morning feeling like I'd had a spiritual experience. It seemed so real to me to be seeing my mum. I was so thrilled that she was out in nature. The last time I saw her was when I had to identify her in a morgue. She was so cold and lifeless. It's sort of cruel that I have that as my last memory of her. In my dream, it almost felt like she had been reborn and was enjoying every moment in her field of flowers.' Kerry turned to look out the window, and a tear slid down her cheek. I passed the box of tissues across to her. 'I'm sorry. She has been gone for six years now. You'd think I would have come to terms with her death.'

'There is no expiry date for grieving. You will love your mum until the day you die. Death creates a hole in your heart that shrinks a little with time but it never fully heals. Your mum is alive in your memories and dreams, so they should be cherished.'

Kerry nodded as she wiped at her eyes. 'Thank you.'

The day dragged on. I had two cancellations and instead wrote my magazine column. I expectantly waited for a knock on the door from a courier delivering flowers, but when at the end of the day I still hadn't received any I was surprised. Maybe they were waiting at home.

I got home to a curious cat who wanted to pounce all over my feet, but there was still no sight of flowers, not even an up-ended packet of flour which might be construed for the dream becoming my reality. The closest thing I could find to flowers were the drooping dandelions that I had repotted a few days earlier. I certainly didn't have a green thumb; I couldn't even manage to keep weeds alive.

SHATTERED DREAMS

I sat at my desk, frustrated that my next client Amy was running late. I had told Elspeth that I would go visit her on my lunch hour and then I had some beauty appointments arranged, prior to my modeling shoot the next day. I still snorted at the thought that I was going to be paid to model.

Twenty minutes after the allotted time slot, Amy appeared. 'So sorry, the traffic was dreadful.'

I looked out the window. There was no traffic around here at this time of day.

Although I would usually find out a bit about my client, I needed to just cut to the chase. 'Tell me about your dream.'

'Well you see I dream all the time. I rarely sleep, I have dreadful insomnia and then when I dream they are such short dreams that I can often manipulate.'

'That is called lucid dreaming, and it is quite common in insomniacs. It means you are not getting into deep sleep so you are semi-conscious and aware of what your thoughts are. Can you recollect one of these dreams?'

'The other day I had a dream that I was bathing in melted chocolate. It was so sweet and syrupy. While I was in the bath, a handsome man was feeding me chocolate strawberries. I felt so invigorated and yet calm. When I woke I was so disappointed it wasn't real.'

Finally a client with a dream I didn't want to avoid. Hallelujah!

'Melted chocolate symbolizes your sensuality and eating chocolates shows contentment. I would suggest that while your days are busy, you would like your nights to be spent with a special someone. Do you have a partner?'

'Yes. My husband Mick and I have been married for thirty-three years. He was snoring next to me when I had the dream. Don't get me wrong, he is so sweet, but he's tired all the time. He doesn't show me as much affection as he used to, but he shows me that he loves me other ways.'

'Such as?'

'He brings me coffee in bed every morning.'

'No wonder you feel content. You've hit the jackpot there, Amy!'

'Yes, I guess I have.'

'I'm no therapist, but perhaps if you would like to spice up your love life you could go see a sex therapist for some advice. Otherwise, maybe you could take inspiration from your dreams and feed Mick some chocolate strawberries. Maybe he can make your dreams come true.'

Once Amy left, I quickly gathered my things and raced over to visit Elspeth. The bruising around her eye was nearly all gone, and she looked like a new and improved version of herself. I'd never seen her look so independent and happy. Sam had even given her a small indoor plant as a house-warming gift. I just hoped it wouldn't end in tears with a shriveled brown potted plant left on the windowsill to wither and die. I felt bad that I hadn't thought to bring a gift, but together we chose an outfit of my discarded clothes for her to wear for her work trial the following week.

I was amazed at the transformation she had made in such a short time. She almost passed as a working executive. If she could land this job and keep it, she would be on the road to financial independence and could put her past behind her.

'You look amazing Elspeth. I can hardly recognise you as the same woman I met in the soup kitchen weeks ago.'

Elspeth's eyes began to well with tears.

'Don't you cry. You'll make my cry and I can tell you I'm one hell of an ugly crier,' I said laughing.

'I keep catching my reflection and wondering who it is. I've spent so long catching glimpses of myself in shop windows, looking like a homeless bum. I've become so accustomed to being invisible to people and making sure I don't get eye contact so I don't make them feel uncomfortable. It feels so weird that people have started treating me like a normal human being. The other day I walked into a shop and the sales assistant walked my way. I almost expected her to usher me out of the shop or accuse me of stealing. I was shocked when she asked if she could assist me. I actually looked over my shoulder to see if she was talking to someone else. I feel like I've found the old me.'

Tears streamed down my face. 'Oh Elspeth, that's so good.' I hugged her tightly. When I pulled away, I laughed, 'Look at me crying like a baby.' I wiped my eyes and when I removed my hand, a smudge of black mascara coated the back of my fingers. I just knew my face now resembled Alice Cooper. 'I warned you I'm an ugly crier,' I said as I sniffed heavily.

'You're the most beautiful person I know, inside and out.'

'Thank you.'

'I just hope Sam realises how special you are. It would make my day if you had someone to share your life. If there is one thing that I have come to realise over the past few weeks, it is how important human relationships are. People can survive by themselves, but there is no quality of life without others to share this journey. The fact that a wee bairn like you took me in and gave me a new lease on life is proof of how important it is to stay connected with other people. Your gift of believing in me is something I will never forget.'

I continued to blubber like a small child. 'I'm so glad to have helped you.' I swiped my hand across my face again and found there was more black than skin tone on my hands. 'Okay, you need to stop making me cry. I have to go to the beautician and she is going to think that my mother has died.'

'You might start a new makeup trend that will take over the world.'

'I don't think so. Can I use your bathroom to try and get rid of the makeup that is all over my face?'

'Sure. It is the second door on the right. Just knock if the door is closed as Susan might be in there.'

'How is your roommate?' I whispered, in case she was in ear-shot.

'She's nice. Poor thing has had a tough life.'

'Well it is nice that you two get on okay. I hope if I bump into her, I don't scare her. She will wonder who the nutter is that has turned up to visit you wearing Halloween makeup.'

After I wiped away the last remnants of my makeup, I joined Elspeth in the lounge room. 'I'm not sure whether red-ringed eyes look any better than my smudged mascara.'

'You will look normal by the time you arrive there. Now you had better get a hurry on. You don't want to be late for your pampering.'

As I walked to my car, I realised that Elspeth hadn't offered me any chocolate. Not that I expected her to give me chocolate as a sign of gratitude, it was just that I was sure it wouldn't take long until the chocolate from my client Amy's dream would mysteriously enter my life.

I raced to the beautician, arriving a few minutes late. She escorted me into a room with a bright neon ring light and looked at my face from all angles before proclaiming I needed a lot of work. I didn't think that bode well for my photo shoot the next week. What if I turned up and they took one look at me and then choked, saying I wasn't what they were after? I really had to start saying no to people more often. Particularly to handsome models that wanted me to do stupid things like acting and modeling.

The beautician clarified, moisturized and pasteurized my face, or maybe that was pasteurized milk in my tea – I'm not quite sure. Anyway, within two hours she had left me with sculpted brows, a hairless top lip, soft supple skin and a slightly irritated right eye from the dying solution she had used to dye my already dark eyelashes. She held up a mirror to show me the results of my makeover. I couldn't really see out of my right eye, but my left eye thought I looked okay, or at least I would once the redness died down, where the wax had ripped the hair follicles from my face.

As I paid the bill, I anticipated I'd be offered a chocolate, but there were none forthcoming.

When I stopped to get groceries, I half expected the checkout chick to hand me a free sample chocolate. It was always so intriguing to find out how a dream was going to materialize.

I made sure I bought some strawberries, in case I suddenly found a pot of melted chocolate mysteriously delivered to my front door.

When I got home Marmie was clearly excited to see me. Although it was a bit lonely without Elspeth, it was nice to be Marmie's primary focus once more.

I made dinner and ate it watching television, anticipating a knock on the door any moment to discover Sam there on bended knee and a love heart-shaped box of chocolates. The knock didn't come.

I washed and dried my plate, as I'd embraced being the cleaner version of myself. I then searched the cupboard for any trace of chocolate. The only thing resembling chocolate that I could find was a chocolate worming drop for Marmie.

As much as I wanted to know how the dream was

going to play out, at that stage I really was just craving chocolate and was desperate for its sweet taste.

Maybe the bath was the key. I ran the bath, worried that there might be a broken pipe and the water coming out might resemble the colour of chocolate, but the warm water was clear and inviting. Eventually I gave up on eating chocolate and instead decided to soak in the bath. My muscles relaxed, and I found myself feeling sleepy. I dried off and snuck into bed, trying to not disturb Marmie who had stretched out across two thirds of the bed.

The next morning I was perplexed. The two previous days had passed without the dreams materializing. Damn it, they were the only dreams I'd heard so far that I wanted to happen. I felt cheated.

MODEL IN THE MAKING

The day before the shoot, I went to the nail salon to get a manicure. I wasn't sure what colour would best suit being a model, so I chose a neutral shade of pink. The thought of having to stand in front of a photographer for hours filled me with dread. I was usually the person behind the camera, or if I was in a group selfie, I held the camera so I could crop half my head out of the shot. I made a mental note to start saying no to people. It was too late now to back out of the shoot and I guess as Levi saved my life, the least I could do is return the favour by modeling for him.

Having had issues with wet nail polish in the past, I had cleverly pre-paid for my manicure so my polish would stay in perfect condition. As I reached the carpark, I reached into my bag to retrieve my car keys, and dragged my semi-dry/still wet nails over the lining in my handbag, leaving a lovely pale pink stripe in its wake. I looked at the lumpy nail polish and sighed. I made another mental note to get a car with keyless entry so I wouldn't mess up future manicures.

Elspeth had been working at the nursing home for a few days, so I decided to drop in to see how she was going.

I knocked on the door and waited for Elspeth to greet me. I stood staring at the garden beds, smiling at the sight of bees buzzing happily around the daisy bush that was in full bloom, with petite white flowers. Maybe instead of trying to keep dandelions, I could attempt to have real flowers grow at my place.

I knocked again, rapping harder to get her attention.

Eventually I heard someone shuffling towards the door. A muffled voice yelled, 'I'm coming.'

When the door opened I was surprised to see another woman. She was a similar age to Elspeth, and she squinted at me, looking like I had just woken her.

'Sorry to disturb you. You must be Susan. I'm Maggie. I came to see Elspeth, if she is home.'

'No worries. I do shift work, so I was just trying to get some sleep. Elspeth ain't here. I think I saw her down by the park in town when I was on the bus comin' home.'

My heart sank. Why would Elspeth be at the park? Maybe the job hadn't worked out, and she had hit rock bottom again.

'Thanks. I'll go see if I can find her.'

Susan nodded and closed the door.

I drove directly to the park and walked towards the area that I had previously found Elspeth. The area under the tree was empty. I slowly walked around the park. Just as I was about to give up hope of finding her, I heard her distinctive laugh. I turned to see her huddled under a blanket with a man with a long grey dreadlocked beard.

'Elspeth,' I called.

'Hello luv,' she replied. 'This is Harry.' Turning to Harry she said, 'Harry, this is Maggie, the angel I was telling you about.'

Harry placed his brown paper bag encased bottle down and extended his hand out to shake.

Smiling, I shook his hand with gusto. 'Nice to meet you, Harry.'

'What are you doing in this neck of the woods?' Elspeth asked.

'I went to visit you at your home and your housemate told me she saw you down here. Is everything okay?'

'Everything is better than okay.' She lifted her own brown paper encased bottle and clinked it against Harry's.

'How is the job going?' I probed.

'It's great. All the feedback has been good. I think that they will offer me the job.'

'That's great news,' I replied.

'Tis,' Elspeth said smiling.

'Um, so why are you back here at the park and not at home?'

'I came down to have a drink with my mates. These people here are my tribe. I once told Harry that if I ever got back on my feet, I'd buy him a drink and that's what I did today. We are having a celebratory drink.' She took another swig from her bottle.

'Oh right,' I replied, not knowing what to say.

'Darl, you might be able to take a woman out of the park, but you can't take the park out of the woman,' Harry said, laughing.

'Maggie, I'm so grateful for all you've done for me. I really love my new home and job, but I've missed these guys, and I wanted to see how they were doing. Remember the other day when I was talking about human relationships? Well it occurred to me that I need to make time to still see my mates. It's as important for me as it is for them.'

'Well, I won't intrude any more. Make sure you get home safely, okay? And let me know if you get the job.'

'I will,' Elspeth said, before taking another swig of wine.

As I walked away, I was shocked at how easily Elspeth had fitted back in with her old life, but also at how much her life had changed since I had met a few weeks prior. If she was able to lift the spirits of other people who were at rock bottom, maybe she could make a positive impact on them. I just hoped it didn't work the opposite way, and she got dragged back down. I knew that it was her life to live but after having stuck my neck out to help her, I desperately hoped that she never found herself destitute again.

The following morning, I was so nervous I couldn't eat. Levi had sent me a text with the details for the shoot. Maybe there would be chocolate croissants on set, or maybe that only happened for supermodels.

I arrived at the warehouse studio and was warmly welcomed. The photographer ushered me in. 'The plus sized model is here,' he called out.

The client, a woman the same size as me, arrived and shook my hand.

'We were so happy when Levi recommended you. I've been campaigning for months to try out a larger model. Someone the masses can relate to.'

I wasn't sure if I should feel honoured or insulted.

A skinny assistant, with pale pink hair and large black-framed glasses, handed me some clothes on hangers. 'Size 14, right?'

I couldn't believe she just announced it to the world. 'Uh huh.'

'The change room is over there and then we will do hair and makeup over by the window.'

I changed into a floaty floral dress with a tailored jacket in a deep emerald that matched the foliage on the dress.

As I sat in a chair by the natural light of the window, I closed my eyes. The whole time I was in the chair I was going through my mantras of 'you can do this,' 'you are beautiful,' and 'you deserve chocolate.'

By the time the makeup artist and hairdresser had finished, I couldn't recognise my reflection. I had dark glossy curls, a youthful glow (which given I was only in my twenties was probably to be expected) and my green eyes were popping.

I stood on a white paper backdrop and as the camera clicked and the flash popped, for a moment I felt like one of the beautiful people. I laughed, flicking my hair from side to side, staring down the barrel of the lens. The photographer only gave me minor cues, like, 'put your hand on your waist to slim down your tuck shop lady arms.'

By the end of the shoot, I was euphoric, having successfully completed my first modeling contract. It actually wasn't that bad and for a moment I considered whether I should put my details on the books for Levi's agency to pick up more modeling work.

As I went to leave, the client came to thank me for my efforts. 'The shots look great. You know we really appreciate you doing this. It is difficult to find models willing to have their image associated with incontinence pads. It's nice to put a younger face to women of all ages that suffer this problem.'

What. The. Actual. Hell. Bloody Levi hadn't told me what the ads were for. How embarrassing! And now there was no way out. They had the photos and god knows what they had in mind for the ads.

I instantly changed my mind about listing my name as a model at Levi's agency. Lucky he had saved my life; otherwise I might have been tempted to end his, after this debacle.

DREAM COME TRUE

I may have now been the poster girl for incontinence pads, but hopefully no one I knew would ever see those ads. I prayed that they would only litter nursing home's monthly newsletters. At least my hair and makeup were done, just in time to meet Sam's mum that night. I really wanted to make a good impression, but I was worried that she would already dislike me as I may be seen as a threat to her plan to get Sam to move back to Fiji.

I didn't have time to worry about that as I rushed to the office to see my next client. I looked at her name in my diary, Sarah Chakrabarti. I'd googled the surname when she had booked to determine what nationality she would be and whether her ethnicity would affect the interpretation of her dreams. Being an Indian surname, I'd consulted a website on Hindu dream symbolism, to ensure I gave her the best possible explanation of her dreams.

A quiet knock on the door drew my attention away from my computer. A petite lady with a blonde pixie cut, blue eyes and a deep tan stood in the doorway.

'Hello?' I said. Surely this wasn't my next client. She wasn't in a sari, with black hair and a red dot on her forehead.

'Are you Maggie?' she asked.

I nodded. 'Yes.'

She walked towards me, 'Hi, I'm Sarah.' A small smile played on her lips as she registered my confusion.

I shook her hand. 'Sorry I was expecting you to look Indian.'

'I often get that. My husband has Indian heritage.'

I was embarrassed that I had lodged a stereotype in my mind of what she would look like.

'Please take a seat. Would you like tea or coffee?' I always used this ploy to buy time to have a chat to find out a bit about a new client.

'White tea, no sugar, please.'

I turned on the kettle.

'So, you have a husband of Indian descent. Do you have any children?' She looked to be in her early fifties. Was it a mistake to assume she might have kids given I was wrong with my other assumptions that day?

'Yes, I have three sons. One has moved out of home and the other two are still at school.'

'I always wonder whether a parent has a sense of loss, or relief, when a child leaves home. I think my parents were relieved.'

'It is a mixture. I believe you need to give your children wings to fly, but then let them know they will always have a base to return to.'

'That sounds like great advice.' I made the tea and placed it in front of Sarah. 'Do you work?'

'Yes, my husband and I are both doctors. It is how we met.'

'I take my hat off to you. You sound like a superwoman.'

Sarah laughed. 'Not at all. I just do what I can to help the community stay healthy and well and at the same time, try to stay sane with my sons being so busy all the time.'

'Do you think any of your sons will follow you

into medicine?'

Sarah snorted. 'If you ask them, they all want to be professional sportsmen but they will each find the right path for them and if they don't, then they will hopefully learn from their experiences.'

'You sound like a very wise woman.' I took a sip of my tea. 'So Sarah, would you like to tell me about your dream?'

'My dream was about my eldest son. I dreamt that he found a sweet girl and fell head over heels in love with her. So much so that he wanted me to meet her so he could get my seal of approval.'

'Right.' I searched my memory bank for symbolism I could relate to this dream. It wasn't a dream of a baby or small child or of her falling in love. I took another sip of my tea to gather my thoughts.

The door to my office opened and Sam was standing there. I looked at my watch. I had obviously got the time for our dinner mixed up. It was almost five pm, but I thought we were meeting at his place after I finished work.

'Excuse me for a moment Sarah. Hi Sam, I'm sorry, I'm just in the middle of a session with a client. Is everything okay?'

Sam walked over and planted a kiss on Sarah's head and grinned widely. 'Yep, everything is great.'

My stomach flipped. Sam had lost his mind, and I wasn't sure how my client would react to his bizarre behaviour.

Sarah smiled up at Sam.

I changed my perspective – maybe I had lost my mind. I was totally confused.

Sam laughed, 'I see you've met Mum.'

Now I was totally baffled. Sam with his chocolatey brown skin and wavy black hair couldn't possibly be Sarah's son. He had Fijian parents. I shook my head, hoping to clear it. 'What?'

The two of them laughed raucously as I stared from one of them to the other.

'I don't understand.'

Sarah reached out and grabbed my hand. 'In my mid twenties I travelled to Fiji on holiday and fell in love with a gorgeous Fijian man, Abraham Telavatu. We married and had Sam together, but tragically Abraham drowned when working on a dive charter. After Sam moved to Australia, I fell in love with one of my colleagues, Arun, and we had two sons together Josiah and Isaac.'

The pieces of the puzzle were starting to fall into place.

'Sam, why didn't you tell me your mum was Australian? I thought she was Fijian.'

Sam laughed. 'It never occurred to me to mention Mum was Australian. As long as I've known her she has always lived in Fiji. I don't think of her as a particular nationality, she's just my mum.'

'I would never have picked your mum to be a blonde Australian, living in Fiji, married to an Indian.' I turned to Sarah, 'You're too petite to have a bulking big son like Sam.'

Sarah chuckled. 'He obviously takes after his father. Sam was taller than me by the time he was eleven.'

Sam walked around next to me. 'I'm sorry if this has totally thrown you. We thought it would be fun for mum to get to meet you and see how adorable you are before we have dinner tonight.'

I playfully punched him in the arm. 'Thanks for stitching me up. I wanted to be on my best behaviour to meet your mum and now I don't get another chance to make my first impression.'

'Don't worry; you impressed me when you

called me a superwoman. But seriously Maggie, you don't need to try to impress me. Like my son, I think you are adorable, beautiful and smart. All the things he told me you were.'

I looked up at Sam to see if this was just another practical joke he and his mum were having at my expense, but instead he was smiling and nodding in agreement.

I stared at Sarah. 'So you didn't really have that dream then?'

'I didn't need to dream it as it is real life. I'm here because Sam cares so deeply for you he has decided to not return to Fiji to live.'

I almost got whiplash as I turned to look at Sam. 'Really?'

His bright white smile beamed at me. 'Really! Maggie, I know I've been holding you in limbo because I didn't want to hurt you, but I've made my decision. I'm going to keep my business here and then travel with the Fijian Olympic rugby team to be their physio. I'm not moving to Fiji. I want to stay here because I really like you and I'd love us to be together.'

I stood up and hugged Sam. 'You're my dream man,' I whispered in his ear.

As Sam stared over my shoulder, he registered the marks on the wall. He held me at arm's length. 'What happened in here? Where is your dream catcher?'

'Well, you know the other day I said I had a bad day; well it was a really bad day. Jason's partner, who by the way turns out to be a fugitive on the run, came to attack me as Jason dumped her after he found out about the cat incident. She went crazy, throwing things around my office and lunging at me with a knife. She slashed the dream catcher and broke it. That's why there are gashes on the wall. I managed to run from the office and she chased me upstairs. Levi managed to grab her, but he got stabbed in the process. Anyway, she was arrested and is apparently now being extradited back to Queensland.'

'Why didn't you tell me she threatened you? You're lucky to be alive.'

I nodded somberly. 'I know. I'm so relieved to know she is going to be living in another state.'

'I wish I had been there for you. Are you feeling okay after that? I'm sure it would have been traumatic.'

'I'm okay, but something weird has happened. My clients' dreams have stopped being converted into reality.'

'Really?'

'Yes, the last two days I've had clients share dreams and really good dreams too, but they haven't come true.'

Sarah interjected, 'Well not until today.'

I laughed. 'Well technically you didn't have that dream, and you did stage this whole thing, so it probably doesn't count.'

'It must have been that the dream catcher was trapping your client's dreams and then expelling them onto you. I feel like you really missed the opportunity to exploit that. How unlucky. Just think how rich you could be now.'

I shook my head. 'I'm relieved it's gone. I'm not feeling at all unlucky, particularly since I know you're staying now.'

Sarah stood up. 'I'm going to leave you lovebirds alone. I'll see you guys back at Sam's house for dinner at 6pm.'

As soon as Sarah closed the door behind her, Sam tilted my head back and kissed me passionately. When we finally came up for breath Sam smiled at me. 'You look pretty happy.'

'You've just made all my dreams come true.'

Sam chuckled.

'Was that too cheesy?' I asked coyly.

'You know a four cheese pizza, when it has hot melted cheese that goes all stringy and as much as you try to pull a slice away from the rest of the pizza there is still heaps more cheese?'

'Yes,' I responded slowly, as the cogs in my brain tried to keep up.

'Well it was like that but without the pizza base.'

As I tried to make a mental note to tone down the gooey romantic comments, I became distracted by Sam's face looming ever closer to mine.

'Lucky that four cheese is my favourite type of pizza.' He then leant forward and kissed me again, wiping all thoughts from my mind.

The End

THANK YOU

I hope you enjoyed 'Maggie McIntyre is Living the Dream'. If you did, I would really appreciate you leaving a review at Amazon or Goodreads, or recommending the book to a friend, who might enjoy some light and easy reading.

I have to pass on my greatest appreciation to my trusted beta readers, Tammi Watson, Aimee Quinlan, Sally Trethewy, Scott Nicholson and Rachel Woo. Their feedback gave me valuable insight to help me improve this story.

It was a pleasure using Susan Keillor to edit this book. Her professionalism and advice was much appreciated.

My thanks must also go to Alison Brown, from my local independent bookstore, Bookface, for supporting me, by stocking and selling my novels.

Thanks also to my family and friends for their continued support throughout my writing journey.

ABOUT THE AUTHOR

Joanne Nicholson is an Australian author who enjoys boating, exercising, reading, writing, music and spending quality time with family and friends.

Joanne's career began in advertising and marketing. After a hiatus to raise her four children, she owned an indoor play centre, worked in property management and bookkeeping. Joanne gave these up to focus on her passion for writing.

To follow Joanne you can find her at:

Facebook @joannenicholsonauthor

Twitter @jolnicholson

Instagram @joannenicholsonauthor

Or, visit her website: www.joannenicholsonauthor.com

After Tiffany is orphaned on the night of her 18th birthday, she discovers, as the sole heir to her parents' estate, she has inherited a frozen embryo from when they did IVF to have her.

Feeling lost, alone and longing for a sense of family, Tiffany can't bring herself to destroy or donate the embryo. Instead, she decides to be impregnated with her biological twin. A legal battle ensues over whether the embryo is a person or property and the ethics of whether it is acceptable to give birth to your own sibling.

Set in Australia, this contemporary fiction novel is full of emotion, dilemmas and unexpected friendships as Tiffany forges a new life without her parents.

After spending her twenties travelling and living a carefree life, Ruth dreams of getting married and having a family. In her mid thirties and with her biological clock ticking loudly, Ruth goes to extreme lengths to become a mother. She is in shock when she finally gets a positive pregnancy test result back from the doctor, as well as being advised that she is now HIV positive.

With the love and support of her friends and family, she adapts to her new state of being and prepares for the challenges ahead of living with HIV and becoming a single mum.

Set in Australia, this contemporary fiction novel explores the modern day conundrum of internet dating, IVF and raising a child as a single parent.

A memory of Lily's late Mum prompts her to do a past life regression to see if they were linked in a previous life. Although skeptical at first, Lily soon finds herself travelling back through memories of her current life and then her previous life in the town of Bathurst, Australia in the early twentieth century. Lily is surprised to find out she was a male and her Dad in this life was her brother in her past life.

Wanting to confirm the facts of the regression were real, Lily researches the property she saw in her memories and discovers Elizabeth, her little sister from her past life, is still alive. Curiosity leads Lily to contact Elizabeth to see what she is like as an elderly woman and to test whether they have a connection in the present.

When Chloe finds out she has inherited a skill that will allow her to learn to read minds, she is excited to have an insight into what people think and feel. Initially, mind-reading appears to be an amazing gift as Chloe excels at work, using her skill to manipulate clients.

However, Chloe soon comes to the realisation that those people closest to her rarely say what they think. She is heartbroken to find out that her best friend lusts after her husband and that her husband fantasises about other women.

Unable to stop her mind-reading, Chloe is left with the dilemma of how she can live with her new found skill. Chloe's life takes on an unexpected new direction as she adapts to reading minds.

A tropical holiday in Mexico seems the perfect way to celebrate a milestone birthday for four Australian women. Cocktails, sunshine and mariachi bands make this a trip of a lifetime, however their dream holiday turns into a nightmare when they are kidnapped and held for ransom. This short story touches on how each of the girls deals with this traumatic event differently.

When a little old gentleman goes into a bustling café to place an order for coffee he is ridiculed and humiliated for not being able to place his order electronically. Upset, he slams down a tattered old magazine on the counter, telling the crowd that karma will come back to haunt them.

As each person who picks up the discarded magazine reads their horoscope, they are surprised to find that it is accurate – but maybe not in the way they first imagined.

After reading this short story, you may not look at your horoscope in the same way ever again!

This is a work of fiction. Names, characters, businesses, places, events and incidents are either the products of the author's imagination or used in a fictitious manner. Any resemblance to actual persons, living or dead is purely coincidental.

Author: Joanne Nicholson
Editor: Susan Keillor
Book cover design: GermanCreative